What's t... ... *g*
frighten you...

He slowly brushed his f... ...er shoulder. Shivers of uncertainty and pleasure raced along her spine.

"No man frightens me." She kept her face expressionless as he baited her.

His brows arched in mockery, even as his mouth quirked, as though not entirely pleased with her answer. "What does frighten you?" He traced his fingertips down her shoulder to her elbow. "Monsters in the night? Head hunters? The bogeyman?"

"I've learned to contain my fears, to not let them conquer me."

"Have you? How admirable. Just as a good Christian girl should do." His fingers and thumb went to her chin, and he lifted it high as though inspecting something. "Ah, yes. There *is* the sign of victory in those eyes! And yet, every champion has his weakness. What's your weakness, Sarah?"

Before she could answer, his lips were on hers in a kiss meant both to seduce and possess. Almost immediately it turned gentle, tender. Taken by surprise, she didn't fight him. A floodgate of emotions raged through her soul. As abruptly as the kiss came, he ended it. Released his hold on her chin. Stepped back.

Offense gave way to compassion when Sarah saw remorse infuse his eyes.

"Forgive me." His plea was no more than a croak.

Before she could respond, he turned on his heel and left her. Sarah watched him go, thrashing the bushes out of his way, his step heavy and swift as he headed for the beach as though he were the one now being hunted.

Thoughts in a whirlwind, she returned to her father's hut. Of all the emotions Bill's unexpected kiss evoked, the one that alarmed her most was the longing she'd felt for it never to end.

PAMELA GRIFFIN lives in Texas and divides her time among family, church activities, and writing. She fully gave her life to the Lord in 1988 after a rebellious young adulthood and owes the fact that she's still alive today to an all-loving and forgiving God and a mother who prayed that her wayward daughter would come "home." Pamela's main goal in writing Christian romance is to encourage others through entertaining stories that also heal the wounded spirit. Please visit Pamela at www.Pamela-Griffin.com.

Books by Pamela Griffin

A Gentle Fragrance

Pamela Griffin

Heartsong Presents

A huge thanks to Tamela Hancock Murray and Jill Stengl, for staying near their computers during the onslaught of chapters and for getting back critiques to me in record time. Your faithfulness overwhelms me, ladies. Also, another huge thanks to my mom, whose loving help has pulled me through more than once. Thanks to all who helped with this project. As always, dedicated to my Lord and Savior, who does not look upon the former things, but creates a new beginning for all who come to Him.

A note from the Author:
I love to hear from my readers! You may correspond with me by writing:

Pamela Griffin
Author Relations
PO Box 721
Uhrichsville, OH 44683

ISBN 1-59789-133-9

A GENTLE FRAGRANCE

All scripture quotations are taken from the King James Version of the Bible.

All of the characters and events in this book are fictitious. Any resemblance to actual persons, living or dead, or to actual events is purely coincidental.

Our mission is to publish and distribute inspirational products offering exceptional value and biblical encouragement to the masses.

PRINTED IN THE U.S.A.

one

The South Pacific, 1921

If he ever returned to New York, he was a dead man.

Bill Thomas stood at the stern of the ship, his pensive gaze sweeping the deep blue ocean and the globe of an orange sun setting beyond a distant island. Here at sea, they would never find him. Yet this time, that reminder did little to steady his nerves.

As he stood watch, the fire of the sky faded to dull blue and violet. The sea grew ever darker, save for two ripples of crimson forming a trail of light toward the horizon. His mind traveled a course all its own, reliving the peril of two years ago.

Somehow, he'd succeeded in escaping Manhattan and gaining employment as a sailor on this vessel. New York remained a distant memory. But even after sailing the high seas for fourteen months, he couldn't shake the fear of reprisal that often had him looking over his shoulder. His brother, Brent, would say the hounds of heaven were giving chase and the guilt for Bill's past crimes was finally catching up to him. Maybe Brent was right, though ironically this time Bill's escape had nothing to do with his own folly.

With his hands spaced wide apart and gripping the rail, he leaned forward. In the last glimmer of evening light, he noticed the water break and white spray shoot upward. Within seconds, a dolphin arced above the surface, outlined for a moment against the horizon, then disappeared back into the water to repeat the process. The antics of the playful water animal brought a faint smile to Bill's face.

Yes, he was a fugitive, but he couldn't have picked a better spot in which to find sanctuary. This chain of South Sea Islands held a mystery that intrigued Bill each time the ship anchored near them to deliver and collect goods. The expansive sea offered secrets of continual interest. Life could be worse.

A thud struck the deck behind him, louder than the creaks of timbers and slap of waves hitting the hull. Bill sharply pivoted to look. In the shadowy twilight, he couldn't make out any sign of life on board. Only the usual ropes, barrels, and crates. A full moon rose above the waters, and faint stars dotted the sky, but he wished for more light.

"Ahoy, who goes there?" Slowly he headed in the direction he'd heard the noise.

No response.

Hair bristled at the back of his neck, but he continued forward as duty demanded.

After investigating the area to find it empty, he scolded himself for allowing old fears to harass him once again. He was free of all that had happened in New York. There was no reason to keep dwelling on those days.

Returning his attention to the dolphin, he squinted to see the sea creature and noted that it now jumped closer to the ship, its splashes easily heard. The sun was only a memory; the sky the color of faded ink.

A thick arm grabbed Bill around his upper chest from behind while something razor-sharp sliced into his ribs. Vision clouding from pain, Bill barely made out the terse words whispered in his ear, "Sleep with the fish. Compliments of Vittorio."

Nausea rose to his throat as his attacker pushed him over the rail. The sea rose up to meet him as his wounded body splashed into the ocean. Thrashing his arms to keep afloat despite the searing pain, Bill spat out salty water. "Help!" His plea came faint. He choked down a breath, certain it would be his last. His blurry focus latched onto the bright moon shining like a beacon.

"Dear God, save me!" he cried through water that invaded his mouth and nose and strangled his words.

The ship sailed farther away. He struggled to stay conscious, to stay afloat, but he could feel his body weaken and his mind fade with every slosh of the waves against his face.

He was going to die.

ᴥ

Sarah opened her eyes and sat straight up in her rope hammock. It rocked back and forth with the motion, and she caught a startled breath. What had awakened her? A sense of foreboding, as if something had happened or was about to happen, plagued her mind and spirit.

She swung her legs over the side, gripping the hammock to steady herself. The moon's glow washed the inside of the thatched hut with brilliant white light. Her father's form lay inert in the hammock across the room. His loud snores proved he was breathing and well, so the danger didn't lie there. She looked out the square hole of the window, her focus going to the moon etched on a blue-black canvas of sky spangled with stars.

The urgency to go outside overwhelmed her, and she walked out the door.

A warm scented breeze caressed her face and body and stirred the coconut palm fronds as she took the familiar pathway. She could walk it even if there were no moon by which to see. The village path was to her right, but she felt the strong impression to go left. Standing high upon a cliff, she surveyed this edge of her island world and noticed movement in the ocean near the beach. Moonlight illumined the waters.

A villager's boat? At night? All the fishermen returned with their catch hours ago. While she watched, her eyes widened. That was no boat!

She raced down the path leading to the empty beach, not stopping when her feet reached the sea's warm, foamy waters. Splashing through, she continued as fast as her legs could move against the press of hindering water. When it surrounded her waist, she dove into the next shallow wave and began swimming with skill, matching that of the dolphin to which someone clung—a man, she could see as she swam nearer.

"I will help you," she called in her native tongue, but he didn't respond. Grabbing his arm in order to shift his inert body toward her, she was surprised when he weakly struggled to be free.

"I mean no harm," she tried again.

His eyes closed. He began sliding off the dolphin. She grabbed him before his head went under and wrapped her arm beneath his limp shoulders around the broad expanse of his chest. Awkwardly she swam with her burden, grateful for the waves that helped push her toward land until her feet could again touch the ocean floor. She considered it a blessing that he'd not been near the coral reef farther down the island, for surely if he had, he would have been cut to ribbons. With difficulty, Sarah dragged him, pulling under his arms, onto the packed wet sand of the beach, until she felt sure the ocean wouldn't carry him away again.

From where had he come? His fair features gave testimony to the fact that this was no islander. For the first time she saw a dark stain at the bottom of his striped shirt.

The man was injured!

She dropped to her knees beside him and pushed the material up so she could see. The surf rushed against them, water washing the blood away from a deep wound that marred his side. Once the wave receded, the wound began to flow again, worrying her. If she didn't do something soon, he could bleed to death.

Using what was on hand, Sarah struggled to rip away his shirt from his body to make a bandage, pulling at the tear at the side. He regained consciousness and open dulled eyes. Again he weakly struck out, attempting to fight her off. Surprised, Sarah drew back.

"No," he groaned in the English tongue of her father. "Leave me alone! I didn't kill Marco." He weakened, arms dropping to the sand. His eyes flickered shut. "Didn't. . . doublecross. . .no one." These last words were faint, and Sarah had to bend her ear to his mouth to hear.

Seeing he was again unconscious, she hurried to resume her task and tied the torn material in a knot around his torso. Sarah studied his ashen face, praying he wasn't dead. She pressed her palm against his chest. Relief washed through her when she felt a faint heartbeat.

Knowing she'd done all she could and must now get help, she pushed herself to her feet and sped up the path to her father's hut.

two

Bill opened his eyes. Brightness seared them, and he raised a hand to shield his face, then cried out as fire ripped through his gut. Within seconds, a vision blocked the sun. He wondered if he had died. For surely the form of the woman who'd come to stand near him was that of an angel.

She wore her black hair loose, past her hips. A breeze from somewhere ruffled wisps of it over bare shoulders and arms. Her feet were also bare, and she wore a bright red sarong covered with white flowers. Did angels wear such finery?

He shifted and gave another muffled cry. The vision knelt and laid her slender hand against his shoulder. "You must lie still. You were wounded and feverish, but my father and I are taking care of you. You have been with us three days."

Her husky-soft voice soothed, and he relaxed back onto what he now realized was a straw mat. His throat felt dry. "Water," he rasped.

She left and soon returned with a wooden dipper. Slipping her hand behind his neck, she helped him raise his head. Cool and pure, the water slid down his throat.

"Where am I?" he asked when he could talk.

"On our island in my father's hut. He's a missionary to the people here."

He took note of her clear skin, a pale pecan-brown. Her almond eyes were brown also, but with golden lights in them, and her lashes were thick and black. Her delicate bone structure, lush thick hair, and slender carriage reminded him of the many beautiful island women he'd seen, but her coloring was too fair to be a native's.

10

"What's your name?" he whispered.

"Sarah."

The door to the hut opened. A tall, thin man walked inside, his scraggly beard, mustache, and hair salt-and-pepper gray. His swarthy skin was almost as tanned as Bill's arms and torso. Like the woman, he wore no shoes, though his trousers and shirt looked American.

"Ah, good," he said. "Our patient is awake." Green eyes twinkled in a weathered face. He set a straw basket onto a carved oak desk, oddly out of place in this primitive hut.

Sarah gracefully rose to her feet. "Father." She kissed his cheek and took the basket to a table. He walked closer to Bill and squatted beside his mat.

"Welcome to our modest home. I am Josiah LaRue, sent as a missionary from America to this island more than twenty years ago. And you are?"

"Bill." Uncertain of whom to trust, he didn't give his last name.

"Well, Bill, consider yourself fortunate. If that dolphin hadn't brought you here and my daughter hadn't been at the beach to bring you to land, you would be a dead man. If not by drowning, then by sharks. The Lord must have a great mission in mind for you."

Josiah's mention of God made Bill uneasy. Why should God save him? He'd done nothing right in his sorry existence. The man's words fully sank in.

"A dolphin brought me?"

"Yes. Queerest thing I ever heard of, but Sarah was a witness. The dolphin carried you to the island. I imagine it's the same one that's become something of a pet of hers. In my forty-eight years on this earth, I've learned the Almighty can and will use anything to achieve His purposes. Once He caused a donkey to speak to a man named Balaam, so I suppose He could and would use a friendly dolphin to help rescue a lost seafarer."

Bill remembered. He had cried out to God to save him. Just as he thought he would sink to the ocean floor, the dolphin he'd been watching from the ship glided near him, slowly circling. Desperate, he'd grabbed its dorsal fin. The dolphin had nosed under, lifting Bill partly out of the water, and he'd held on. Bill remembered little of what happened next.

"Did you fall overboard?" Josiah asked. "I assume from your clothing that you're a sailor."

"Yes. I fell overboard." Bill left it at that. The less these people knew, the better.

The man was quiet a moment, his intent gaze causing Bill discomfort.

"You must have hit something sharp on your way down," Josiah said. "The gash in your side was deep, but with my daughter's knowledge in healing herbs and the little suturing I've learned, it's on the mend now." He straightened to a stand. "You're welcome to stay with us as long as you like."

"I appreciate that."

Josiah gave a nod. "You must be hungry. Sarah, fix our guest a meal."

"Yes, Father."

Bill looked past Josiah to Sarah. Unsmiling, she steadily regarded Bill. The way she stared made him look away, uneasy. How could she know he was holding back the truth?

❧

Sarah sliced the white meat of a coconut. Each chop of the knife punctuated the truth ringing in her mind. The man called Bill had lied to them. Why? And whom had he thought he'd addressed when he fought her help that night on the beach?

As it had many times, her gaze went to his slumbering form. Never had she seen eyes so light in color, reminding her of shallow turquoise waters, or hair so pale. It grew past his ears and resembled the shade of yellow grasses near the center of the island when the noonday sun hit them. When she'd first seen his hair wet that night on the beach, it had been dark, and she'd been surprised to see the color lighten once it dried. She'd never seen hair do that. Curious, she further studied his face. His profile resembled the picture of an aristocratic prince in a history book of her father's. Yet this man was no prince.

He lay there, frail as a newborn. Bruises marred his stomach and arms, but his muscular torso gave testimony to untold strength. He must be strong to endure what he had. She'd been amazed she was able to drag him from the sea, and he'd survived the stabbing, though certainly that must be in part due to their many petitions to God. Sarah was certain it was a stab wound Bill had suffered, not a "gash" he'd received during his fall into the ocean, as Father suggested.

Two years ago, a boy had been attacked with a knife after a village ceremony. Sarah's father had attended the boy. His wound resembled Bill's, though sadly it was closer to the heart, and the boy died.

"Sarah?"

Her father's muted voice caught her attention. Abandoning the preparation of their meal, she moved to join him where he stood by the open door. He led her a short distance from the hut, into the shade of a coconut palm.

"You are so like your mother, quiet and still, but your eyes reveal your secrets. You're not happy Bill is staying with us."

"I do not trust him." Sarah lifted her palms in a delicate shrug. "Yet what else is to be done? He needs our help. You're a missionary; you cannot turn him out."

"You're right, Sarah. I can't." Her father lifted his gaze to the white clouds in an azure sky, a gesture used when he had something of merit to say. "I sense his wound is not merely of a physical nature. The fearful words he yelled to you that night prove that. After talking with him, I sense a spiritual struggle similar to what I endured after your mother died. It's my duty as God's chosen servant to help this young man in whatever way possible, in the nurture of both his body and his spirit. Perhaps he was sent to us for that purpose, Sarah."

For a time, neither spoke. Sarah waited until he again looked in her direction.

"If it is your will to have him here, Father, then I will make him feel welcome."

"That's my beautiful girl." He hugged her close with one arm.

Still, unease twined around Sarah when she thought about the man called Bill.

ঽ

Bill surveyed the round hut for what must have been the hundredth time. Never one for inactivity, he was about to go mad from lying flat. According to his mental time track, two days had passed since he'd woken from the fever. A total of five days on this island. The girl and her father treated him well enough and saw to his every need, but he almost wished they'd been cruel to help ease his guilt for withholding the truth and for invading their home. True, the man was a missionary, accustomed to lending aid. But that fact strangely doubled Bill's guilt.

His stoic brother had tried to get him to see the light of Christianity, a light from which Bill had always run fast and run hard. Now he lay stranded, physically helpless, in a missionary's hut. How disgustingly ironic.

Bill looked out the window at a pale square of blue. Palm fronds edged it, and he heard the ocean's surf nearby. Again his mind went to that night aboard ship. Weeks ago, they'd left port with a batch of new sailors, and Bill had been nervous, plagued by the past. One sailor, Guido, used his work as an excuse not to look at Bill, even when Bill addressed the man directly. Had Guido been Bill's assailant?

The crisp sound of a page turning had him shift his focus

to the girl. She sat relaxed in her hammock, reading a book.

"What is there to do on this godforsaken island anyway?" he grumbled.

"You are bored?" she inquired, not looking up from the page. "Would you like one of my father's books to read?"

"No, I would not like one of your father's books to read," he clipped, frustrated. "I want to get outside this hut!"

"Soon, you will heal." She turned another page. "Your wound is better with each day."

He snorted. "That's what you said yesterday. And the day before that."

"Instead of being angry, you should thank God that in His great wisdom He has seen fit to keep you alive."

Bill knew that, but her offhand reminder didn't improve his attitude. "Will you please look at me and at least acknowledge my existence? If I'm to be stuck here, the least you could do is talk to me."

She closed the book, her golden-brown eyes focusing on him. "Very well. What is it you wish to discuss?"

Unnerved by her unruffled manner and steady gaze, Bill averted his attention to the thatched roof. "Tell me about this island. How long have you lived here?"

"I was born here."

"What about the village? Why don't you live there instead?"

He heard her slow intake of breath. "After my mother and her unborn child perished, my father moved from the village to build this hut."

Bill looked her way. "How old were you?"

"Seven."

"You've lived here alone all this time? Why?"

She stood up from the hammock and laid the book on the desk. "My father should be better able to answer your questions when he returns. I must tend to chores."

"Wait!" Bill didn't want to have the hut all to himself again.

"Don't go. I promise to keep my inquiries less personal if you'll stay. And I'll try to be nicer."

She hesitated.

"Cross my heart," Bill said, making the motion with his right hand.

"Cross your. . . ?" Her words trailed off, confused.

"Never mind. Really, I'd like to hear more about your island, so I'll know what to expect once I'm on my feet."

She tilted her head as if considering his request. "I will tell you what you wish to know. On one condition."

"Condition?" This couldn't be good.

"You are recovered enough to sit at our table. Tonight, instead of sleeping, you will listen to my father read the words from the Holy Book. It would please him. On this condition only will I remain and tell you about our island."

Bill grimaced. What she asked wasn't so much, he supposed, though he didn't look forward to the prospect. Agreeing to commit to an hour or more of sure drudgery might be worth it to spend time in her company and learn about this place that would be home until the next ship arrived.

"All right, doll. You got yourself a deal."

"A deal?" Her brows lifted. "This is a yes?"

"Yeah."

She nodded once, as graceful as a princess acknowledging one of her subjects. Pulling her thigh-length hair over one shoulder, she took a seat near his mat. All her movements were graceful, fluid. Again he became entranced by her beauty, then by her words as time slipped into some invisible slot and she opened up to him the mysteries of her island.

three

Sarah was confused. Naturally, it pleased her that Bill had agreed to take part in hearing her father read from the Bible, but she couldn't help feeling his motives were suspect. Perhaps it was the look in his eyes when she caught him watching her, as if he lay in wait like one of the sharks who prowled the waters. Uneasy around him, she looked for excuses to be absent. Conversely, she felt a pull toward him she couldn't explain.

By the light of the candles, Sarah sneaked glances Bill's way. The first two nights he'd listened to the gospel, he'd seemed indifferent, enduring the hour. But tonight, his eyes were alert, his expression tense as he watched her father.

After the book closed, a crackling silence reigned.

"I don't understand," Bill said at last. "Paul helped capture and kill Christians, and God chose him?"

"Yes, another wonderful example of God's saving grace. We're all sinners; all of us deserve hell and damnation. But because of a loving Father, we have assurance of salvation through our Lord and Savior, Jesus Christ."

Frowning, Bill looked out the window. After a moment, he stood. "I need air." He walked through the door, moving more easily than before, yet his actions were slow, stilted.

"You should go to him."

Stunned, Sarah regarded her father. "I? Why should I go to him?"

"Because he'll listen to you."

Amazement gave way to incredulity.

"Speak with him," her father urged. "He turns a deaf ear

toward me, and I've noticed he listens to you."

She didn't know where her father had gotten that impression. If anything, Bill argued with her on a continual basis.

"I'll do as you ask," she said, rising from her mat. *But I'll not like it.*

"You're a true credit to a missionary, Sarah."

Sarah pondered his words. She'd been trained to be subservient to her father as her authority. At the same time, her mother's sister taught her to rely solely on an inner source for strength. Her father called the strength Jehovah. Aunt Lefu called the strength many gods. Sarah did not know what to call it. She believed in the Almighty God, of whom her father preached. Likewise her aunt spoke of the island gods. Sarah had attended village rituals, seen the people's devotion. Was their homage and commitment without basis? Did only one God exist?

She found Bill standing on the cliff where she'd stood seven nights ago, looking out to sea. As on that night, the moon hung low, and a hibiscus-scented breeze stirred the warm air.

Hearing her approach, he glanced over his shoulder, then back out to sea.

"You believe in all your father says?" Bill's question was abrupt, his voice taut.

"I believe there's a God, and Jesus is His Son."

He turned fully to look at her. "From the way you said that, I sense some hesitance on your part."

"There is much yet I don't understand."

"And here I thought you and your kind had all the answers."

When she didn't respond to his caustic remark, he stepped closer. She tensed, again reminded of the shark. The look in his eyes seemed dangerous.

"What's the matter, pretty Sarah? Do I frighten you?" He

slowly brushed his fingertips along her hair, down to her shoulder. Shivers of uncertainty and pleasure raced along her spine.

"No man frightens me." She kept her face expressionless as he baited her.

His brows arched in mockery, even as his mouth quirked, as though not entirely pleased with her answer. "What does frighten you?" He traced his fingertips down her shoulder to her elbow. "Monsters in the night? Head hunters? The bogeyman?"

"I've learned to contain my fears, to not let them conquer me."

"Have you? How admirable. Just as a good Christian girl should do." His fingers and thumb went to her chin, and he lifted it high as though inspecting something. "Ah, yes. There *is* the sign of victory in those eyes! And yet, every champion has his weakness. What's your weakness, Sarah?"

Before she could answer, his lips were on hers in a kiss meant both to seduce and possess. Almost immediately it turned gentle, tender. Taken by surprise, she didn't fight him. A floodgate of emotions raged through her soul. As abruptly as the kiss came, he ended it. Released his hold on her chin. Stepped back.

Offense gave way to compassion when Sarah saw remorse infuse his eyes.

"Forgive me." His plea was no more than a croak.

Before she could respond, he turned on his heel and left her. Sarah watched him go, thrashing the bushes out of his way, his step heavy and swift as he headed for the beach as though he were the one now being hunted.

Thoughts in a whirlwind, she returned to her father's hut. Of all the emotions Bill's unexpected kiss evoked, the one that alarmed her most was the longing she'd felt for it never to end.

❧

Bill stared at the crested waves sweeping the barren beach,

his eyes seeing little. Annoyed frustration with himself and with these religious-minded people had goaded him to move forward, to break through Sarah's aloof barrier with an earth-shaking kiss. But he was the one who'd felt the earth move beneath his feet. And he didn't like what was happening to him.

When his lips pressed against her soft ones, the desire to strike out instantly vanished. As quickly as the kiss altered something indefinable inside Bill, so also came the realization that he didn't want to change Sarah. At that split second the kiss became genuine, no longer a trap he'd designed to cause her to fall off her throne of cool detachment.

He released a breath fraught with aggravation. He had to get off this island. What kind of man was he that he would try to seduce the chaste daughter of the holy man who'd opened his home to him, cared for him, shown him nothing but graciousness?

The worst kind of man.

That kiss not only opened his eyes to the discovery that he preferred Sarah just as she was, but it unearthed the realization that he didn't like himself. And he wasn't the type comfortable with inward examination. Only since he'd come to the island had he analyzed his motives.

Bill wasn't sure what he believed about God, but each day that passed in the missionary's presence brought Bill closer to the plateau to which both the missionary and his daughter were trying to take him. If Bill did accept what they told him, how could he then face himself? His sins were too great and too dark to count. To acknowledge a God and to believe in His Son would push Bill to a point from which there was no return and from where there was no escape. No more running.

The thought was almost more terrifying than being hunted by criminals.

Finished with the wash, Sarah cradled the basket of wet linens under her arm and retraced her steps uphill. The sand burned her feet, and she carried a great banana leaf above her head as a sunshade to block out the sun. The air seemed sleepy as it always did this time of day, any sound unusually loud and misplaced. Many villagers had retreated into the shade of their homes to sleep, but Sarah felt restless.

Catching sight of Bill ahead, standing between two palms and staring out to sea, she hesitated. For the past week he'd steered clear of her, and while his erratic behavior confused, oddly it also disappointed. In the nighttime, she lay awake in her hammock and relived his kiss; in the mornings, she pushed it from her mind.

He turned upon hearing her footsteps rustle in the grass but didn't move away as he'd done every other day this week when he caught sight of her. Instead, he waited until she drew near. Without a word, he took the basket from her, and together they continued up the path. Silence thickened between them, broken only by the sound of the surf upon the beach and the gulls' mewling cries.

He glanced at her, then back up the path. "I'm not a decent man, Sarah. Where I come from, I'm not even considered a good man."

She gave time for his heavy words to settle before she spoke. "There is no one who's truly good, according to Father. All men are evil or have evil thoughts. The goodness must come from without, from relying on God. No one owns true goodness unless they know its Source."

He released a pent-up breath. "You make it sound so simple."

"It is. Father says the problem with many accepting salvation lies in the fact that people want to complicate what should be kept simple. Logic and intelligence confuse, and it is only with the mind and heart of a child one can understand."

He halted, turning on her. "*You* confuse me, Sarah. You speak with such conviction, even if you are only parroting your father. But I've watched you. I followed you last evening."

Sarah's face flushed hot. Bill had spied on her? Her father would be grieved to learn she'd accompanied Aunt Lefu to the temple, something she'd done under great pressure.

"You shouldn't have followed me," she said gravely. "There are dangers of which you know nothing. Things considered taboo to those not of our island."

"Then tell me so I can understand."

His blue-eyed gaze drilled into her, and she looked sideways, to the churning sea. How could she tell him when she herself didn't understand the pull that drew her to her mother's people? During the years her father was ill in spirit, she had drawn close to her aunt, attended tribal rituals. Though she rarely partook of them, she'd opened her ears and mind to the beliefs they reflected.

"How can you expect me to understand, when you yourself seem so lost?" he asked quietly.

She was saved a reply when she heard clicks and squeals and caught sight of a familiar shape breaking above the water. Smiling, she put her hand to his arm. He drew back a little in surprise.

"Come, you must meet Maliu."

"Maliu?"

"Come," she said pulling on his arm that was not holding the basket. "You will see."

ta

Like a child, Sarah almost dragged Bill down the sandy slope and toward the expansive sea, where a rock basin formed a pool. He worked to keep a good hold on the basket. The stab wound had healed over, and her father had removed the thread from the stitching yesterday, but now his side ached due to the fast pace at which she led him.

"Sarah, what's this all about?"

"You'll see." A glint colored her eyes, but it was her mysterious smile that captured his breath. She turned toward the water. "Maliu! Come!"

To his surprise, a blue dolphin broke the ocean's surface, jumping high into the air. The sun glinted off its sleek back as it completed its arc and dove headfirst into the water.

Understanding dawned. "The dolphin that saved my life."

She nodded and took hold of his hand. "Come."

Weary of struggling with the slipping basket, he dropped it to the sand before moving with her toward the rock basin.

He watched as she waded into the water, but he held back. She looked at him.

"Our clothes'll get wet." The explanation sounded lame even to his ears.

She giggled, as if wading into the water fully clothed was an everyday occurrence for her. "They will dry," she teased, pulling him with her.

Bill allowed her to lead him into the frothy, warm water, which lapped at his ankles, then at the knees of his trousers. He'd never seen her like this, so carefree, so happy. The transformation amazed him, and rather than watch the dolphin, which swam closer to receive her friendly pats and soft words, he watched her.

"You can pet him." She looked up. "He won't bite."

Bill patted the area close to the blowhole on the mammal's head, more to please her than the dolphin. Its skin was rubbery and cold. Through intelligent, friendly black eyes it viewed Bill and let out a series of whistles and clicks.

"Maliu likes you," Sarah said in approval.

Bill wondered how she had arrived at such a conclusion. Before he could ask, she swung her legs over the rock and mounted the dolphin as one would a horse. Her frame was slight and the dolphin was long, but her unexpected action put Bill at a loss for words.

As if it had taken this course many times, the dolphin swam with Sarah, circling the shallow waters as she held to its dorsal fin. Her hair hung in a silky curtain, its ends trailing the water. Her face and arms glistened with droplets, and Bill thought he'd never seen a more breathtaking sight as Sarah enjoying a ride on her pet.

She continued laughing as the dolphin neared him. Instead of reentering the pool where he still stood with water past his knees, she slid off the dolphin's back until she was immersed neck-deep in the sea.

"Swim with me?" she asked, treading the water.

The appeal of Sarah almost had him diving in to frolic in the sea beside her. "Too much physical activity isn't good for me right now."

Concern covered her face, and her gaze lowered to his shirt. "You are in pain?"

"Not much. I think I'd rather just sit and watch you." He took a seat on the lumpy lava-like rock shelf that rose inches above the water.

Her smile seemed uncertain, but she gracefully turned her back to him. Her head dipped beneath the water to reappear yards farther out. The loose, knee-length flowered dress she wore didn't impede her movements, and he watched her swim through the water as if she were a mermaid born to it. With every ounce of restraint he held back, though he wished to be there with her, to capture her in his embrace, to hold her, to touch her, and yes, to kiss her again.

He inhaled a shaky breath.

Sarah, Sarah. . .what are you doing to me?

four

"I would like more coconut milk." Josiah leaned back in his chair and held out his cup to Sarah. "Please."

Brows gathered in evident confusion, she looked into the empty container, then at her father. "I will need to gather them. We finished the last with our meal."

"Take your time."

Alert, Bill watched Sarah leave the hut, then turned to look at the missionary. He'd never noticed Josiah had a particular fondness for the ultra sweet, watery milk and suspected a deeper reason hid within the man's directive to his daughter.

Josiah closed his Bible, laid it with infinite care upon the desk, then turned his attention toward Bill. "I have long considered what I'm about to say, and I have a favor to ask."

Bill tensed. Gravity steeled the man's quiet words, putting Bill on the immediate defensive. "I can't promise anything."

"Nor should you without knowing the circumstances." Josiah shifted his gaze to the window and the sea beyond. "When you are ready to leave our island, when a ship comes to take you back to the States, I want you to take Sarah with you."

Bill stared. Surely he couldn't have heard right.

Josiah looked at him, his eyes deadly serious. "This is the only home she's known, and it's time she discovered where my roots lie. I want her to be among other God-fearing Christians, and though there are those here who have come to know Christ, she isn't finding what she needs on this island. I blame myself. Had I been more attentive after my wife died, she might not have sought wisdom from her aunt, who deplores my faith. I only pray any damage done is reversible.

25

You can help me, Bill. You can help me make my peace with God by doing what's best for Sarah."

Bill shot up from his chair and paced to the window. He plowed a hand through his hair. "You don't know what you're asking. You don't know the man I am."

"I've watched you these past weeks. You have a hunger for God, a sincere thirst for knowledge of the truth, and I haven't seen that desire exhibited in many young men. What are you, thirty?"

"Twenty-seven." The reply came automatically, his mind still in conflict with Josiah's request.

Josiah nodded. "God's called you, Bill. You can't escape Him, though you've tried. He saved your life and has chosen you. You're the one holding back, but from your avid questions lately, I don't think it will be much longer until you reach the place of acceptance in Christ."

Bill swung around. "You don't get it—I killed a man. Several men."

Josiah calmly regarded Bill as if he'd just told him he'd swatted a fly.

"Don't you understand?" Bill swung his hands out to the sides. "I'm not worth the trouble."

"Whatever sins lay in your past, God has knowledge of every one of them. Still, He desires you to come to Him, just as He called Saul and gave him a new name and a new mission. He brought you to this island, carried on the back of a dolphin, to recover in a missionary's hut. Do you not see the irony of that?" He chuckled, but Bill didn't feel like laughing. "Would it ease your mind to talk of it?"

Bill closed his eyes. He'd pushed the killings to a far corner of his mind, hoping the memory would rot and disintegrate there. But bad memories never died. "It was either be gunned down or pull the trigger. When someone points a gun at your heart, you don't ask questions."

"I understand."

"Do you?" Bill turned on him. "How can you? Have you ever killed a man in cold blood? Watched as the life seeped from him, as his eyes filled with fear? As he reached up as though begging you somehow to save him, to turn back time—when only seconds before he was the enemy?" He clutched handfuls of his hair. Tore at it while stalking away.

"Yes."

The word came so soft at first Bill didn't think he'd heard correctly.

"Years before I became a missionary, I was a violent young man accustomed to barroom brawling."

Bill swung around to face Josiah.

"During one such brawl, I confronted a peer who'd proven to be an enemy to my selfish desires. I was drunk. I was angry. I knew when to quit but didn't. He kept coming at me, giving punch for punch. I hit him over the head with a chair. He crumpled at my feet. Yet even then, Bill, even then I drew back my fist to finish him off. It was the look in his eyes that stopped me. I'd never seen such fear, such knowing. He reached up—not with his fist—but with his hand outstretched, and clasped my shoulder as if to hold on, as if he were drowning and I was his rope. Something inside me broke. Instead of punching him, I cradled him against me as if he were a child. He died that night. So you see, Bill, I do know."

Gripping silence filled the air. Throat working hard against emotion, Bill swallowed and stared into the cheerless face of the calm man before him. Then without another word, he turned and left the hut.

❧

Twilight's indigo darkness colored the warm air as Sarah returned, her arms laden with coconuts. She couldn't help but feel her father had pushed her out. That he wanted to talk to Bill alone was patently obvious. She had obeyed, yes, but at the same time she'd shielded her true feelings of hurt confusion.

The sound of gasping, as though someone were struggling for air to breathe, made her stop in alarm. Quickly she moved through the trees, her steps silent. She spotted Bill standing at the edge of the cliff, his back to her, the moon silvering his fair hair. The peaceful thunder of the reef echoed beyond. His shoulders shook.

"I'll never understand," he rasped. "Not in a million years. It makes no sense. But who am I to talk about sense? An ex-mobster. A chiseler, a racketeer, and God knows what else. . . ." His chuckle was dry. "Yeah, I guess You do know, don't You? I guess there's no hiding anything from You, though I certainly never tried. Lay all one's cards out on the table—that was always Lucky Bill's motto. So here I am, laying out every filthy card in my deck."

Sarah struggled to hear his next words.

"I have no idea why You'd want the likes of me, but after hearing Josiah's story, I've got no more excuses to run. I've heard what's been read every night for the past two weeks— all about You and what You've done—and I recognize truth for what it is. You got my attention with the dolphin, but being forced to listen really opened my eyes." He let out a self-derisive laugh. "I think I might've recognized the truth when Brent was always preaching it, but I was too much of a tough guy to admit it. I always felt my luck would carry me through, that I didn't need You. But those days are gone. I don't feel so tough or so lucky anymore."

As Sarah watched, Bill dropped to his knees. Her arms tightened around the coconuts. Compassion knotted her throat.

"Josiah said all I had to do was ask You to take over, Jesus. So that's what I'm doing. I've made a huge mess of things, and I have no idea where I'm going. But one thing I'm sure of is that I need You at the helm." He let out a thundering breath in a humorless laugh. "Not sure how that'll work since I've been captain of my ship for so long, doing things my way. But I'm willing to turn the wheel over now. You sure couldn't make things any worse than they already are."

His last words were hoarse, and he bowed his head. Deep sobs shook his body.

Her heart twisted at his brokenness. Something inside whispered for Sarah to go forward, to lay her hand against his shoulder, but she held back, thinking he might not welcome her eavesdropping.

She should have made her presence known, but she hadn't wanted to disturb him. Nor had she wanted to slip away. To secretly share in Bill's decision pleased her. She couldn't recall a time in which a villager's decision for Christ gave her such joy as did Bill's soul-stirring, heart-to-heart talk with God.

Teary-eyed, she watched him several seconds longer, then silently retraced her steps to her father's hut.

ॐ

"Now that I've told you about my home, will you show me your island, Sarah?"

The question startled her, and she turned to study Bill.

"I need the exercise after lying around like a vegetable for so long."

Of its own accord, her gaze flicked down his trim physique; she couldn't see that his convalescence had caused him to suffer in that regard. Embarrassed by the thought, she looked up into his eyes, which regarded her steadily but with none of the predatory animal look that had been in them during his first two weeks on the island.

She glanced away, stacking the last of her father's books on the shelf above his desk. "If you would like."

"I would like very much."

Tenderness laced his voice, making her warm all over. "Then we should go now before the hour comes that I must prepare dinner."

"I'm ready as a rooster."

She looked at him, confused by the terminology as she often was when he used what he called "slang."

He smiled and motioned for her to precede him. "Lead the way."

She cast him an uncertain smile before walking out of the hut. He soon joined her on the path. Why she should feel so awkward, she didn't understand, and she fished for something to say.

"It is difficult for me to see in my mind this Manhattan of which you speak. I cannot imagine buildings so tall they reach to the clouds, nor the absence of so many trees." She looked at the wild panorama of greenery and color all around her. In the boughs of the breadfruit trees, birds let loose shrill cries, and geckos sought their shade. "What do the lizards climb if there are no trees? Where do the birds build their nests?"

Bill laughed and the sound stirred her heart. "Sarah, you're a delight. New York has no lizards, at least not giant ones that run amok like they do here. We have birds, though, and a park in the middle of the city. I guess they make their home there."

"No lizards?" She thought about that. "What about snakes or sharks?"

"Not snakes like here. And the real sharks wear three-piece suits with felt fedoras and carry guns." The smile left his face, and Sarah wished to bring it back.

"Today, I will show you my favorite place on the island." She smiled wide, attempting to rekindle his happiness. "It is where I go when circumstances lie heavy on my heart and I must think."

They walked deeper into the forest while she answered

Bill's frequent questions about the flora, the fauna, and the village. Sarah carefully avoided areas she knew presented dangers, both on the paths over which they walked and in the answers she gave about the people and their customs.

"I can see why you love this island. Do you think you'll ever want to leave?"

His low words made Sarah stare. "I cannot think of leaving, it is all I know. . .and yet. . ."

"Yes?" he prompted when she remained silent.

"I've wondered what lies beyond the sea. My father's books show me much, but they cannot tell me all I wish to know." His question made her uneasy, as did the steady look he gave, and she moved ahead. "It's up here, this place I wish to show you."

As they neared the area, Sarah heard the running of water rushing upon itself and quickened her pace. She rounded the corner and parted the bushes for Bill, watching his expression. His eyes brightened, and he smiled.

"This is great, Sarah. I can see why you'd want to come here."

Pleased with his response, she viewed the lofty wall of bushes that surrounded the clearing, as though nurturing the waterfall and pool nestled within, secreting it away for her sole pleasure. Exotic flowers of ruby, violet, and gold bloomed from the bushes, and the grass lay soft beneath her feet. A natural rockslide stood at the edge, connected to the pool, something she'd enjoyed many times in her girlhood.

"So quiet all of a sudden?" Bill prodded.

"At times, I wish for my childhood back. Things were so uncomplicated then."

"And what's to complicate your life now?" He plucked a red hibiscus from a bush and slid it behind her ear. "There. That's what was missing."

The touch of his fingers on her hair, at her ear, made her breath catch.

"Sarah?" His smile faded, and his eyes grew serious.

She turned away, looking at the pool. She did want him to kiss her; she didn't want him to kiss her. Never had she been so confused. But she didn't want him to think her weak, and she masked her expression before facing him.

"You are right. There is little to complicate my life; I am blessed."

He narrowed his eyes, studying her, when suddenly an ear-splitting screech split the air.

&

Alarmed, Bill looked up, just as a furry animal jumped down on him from the trees, its legs and arms spread wide. "Agh!" He slapped at the creature hanging on to him from behind, trying to wrest its hairy arms from around his shoulders, and was surprised to hear Sarah laughing.

"Mutu, you naughty boy," she said between chortles.

The thing had a hand and began thumping Bill on the head with the flat of it.

"Get it off me!" he demanded.

"Mutu will harm no one. He only wants to be friends."

"This is friendly?" Bill grimaced as the monkey poked its finger into his ear. "Since you appear to be on good terms with the creatures of the animal kingdom, will you please tell it to get off?"

"Mutu, come. You mustn't treat our guest in such a way."

The animal didn't budge, letting out a few *ha-hoo, ha-hoo*s as though arguing with her.

"Perhaps if we walk back to the hut, Mutu will lose interest."

"I've never seen him before," Bill said, striving for patience as he walked with her. "I didn't know the island had monkeys." Now he could feel the inquisitive beast pulling up strands of his hair to study it. At least he hoped that's all it was doing and that it didn't have an appetite for hair.

"Mutu was a freewill gift from a sea captain to my father. But Father will not let him into the hut. He does not like Mutu."

Bill had no problem understanding that viewpoint.

"He sometimes visits me outside when I do chores. And he walks with me over the island when I visit my aunt."

"Do you go to the village often?" Bill tried to talk around the monkey's fingers, which now pulled at his lower lip.

"Mutu, stop that." Her voice rang with quiet authority. To Bill's relief, the monkey unlooped its arms from around him and fastened them around her neck, jumping to her side and wrapping its legs around her. Not pausing in her steps, she looped her arm around its back. "I go as often as necessary."

"Do you act as a nurse there? A teacher?"

She hesitated. "My aunt teaches me many things. I go to learn from her."

Remembering what Josiah said, Bill looked at her. "The beliefs of your mother's people?"

"Do not judge what you do not understand."

"How can I learn the truth if I don't raise questions?" When she didn't respond, he persisted. "Last night, your father read that the Almighty God is a jealous God and there should be no others before Him. Yet isn't that what your relatives do? Put other gods before Him? Even ancestor worship? So why do you take part in it?"

Her step faltered. Bill reached out to grab her, but she quickly regained ground. The monkey chattered at him.

"I do not take part. I go to learn the ancient beliefs and stories of my mother's people. That is all."

"Why? Your father told me that the Bible forbids us to conform to the world's ideals. Wouldn't that same rule apply to life on this island? Tell me. I wish to know, Sarah. How can what your aunt teaches you and what your father teaches you be in any way related?"

She frowned, drawing her brows together. "You must speak of this with my father. I'm not well versed enough in the Word to give you an answer."

Silence settled between them, broken only by the monkey's chattering and the myriad calls of birds in the trees. Once they reached the hut, Sarah made her excuses that she must see to the meal and left with the monkey still riding her hip. Bill watched her go, then turned his attention to her father, who sat about fifty feet away, whittling on something, with his back against the trunk of a palm. Bill moved toward him.

"Did you have a pleasant walk?" Josiah asked, never taking his eyes from the knife he used to cut grooves onto the stick he held.

"You realize that to take Sarah off this island and onto a ship of rowdy sailors for weeks on end is dangerous, don't you?" Bill greeted him. "Have you thought that through? She's beautiful and intelligent, but she's also naive."

"So, you've decided to return and stop running. I'm glad. You'll never be free until you face your fears."

Bill shrugged, as if it were of little consequence, when in reality he'd thought of little else since the night he'd turned to God. The idea of returning had nagged at him until he could no longer push it away. He could lose himself in New York at the reform school where his brother taught. The sea, the islands, they were wild and beautiful, but he missed home.

"I sense you're the type of man to protect others." Josiah's response came lazily. "You'll see to it that no harm comes to Sarah."

"But I can't be with her all the time!" Bill shook his head in frustration. "The vessel on which we sail will probably be a merchant mariner, like the one I was employed on—not a luxury passenger liner with a wide choice of rooms. And those sleeping berths don't have locks on the doors!"

"Well, then. . ." With unhurried ease, Josiah put his

handiwork aside, also laying down his knife. He looked up, regarding Bill steadily. "There appears to be only one recourse."

Bill snorted. "And what's that?"

"Marry my daughter."

five

Marry Sarah? *Marry Sarah?*

Bill struggled with the idea from the moment he had blinked at Josiah after the man had calmly uttered those profound words. Bill then spun on his heel—away from the absurd suggestion—running from it, right up until now, as he sat on the empty beach and stared at the moon. They would probably wonder why he hadn't returned for dinner, but at this moment, Bill didn't care. He had no desire to face either of them.

Yes, she was a beauty, and he was, without a doubt, attracted to her. The thought of holding Sarah in his arms—as his wife—sent warmth soaring through his veins. Her purity, her sweetness drew him. Her intelligence amazed him and at other times needled him. Though he'd never submitted to any authority, he respected the gentle obedience she exhibited toward her father and the loyalty she showed her aunt, even if he didn't understand her reasons for doing what he'd heard was wrong.

But Bill wasn't the marrying type. Never had been. Never would be. That sort of thing was for men like his brother, Brent.

Bill released a pent-up breath and rose from the sand, dusting off his trousers. He picked up a shell and pitched it toward the colorless sea. It disappeared in the silvery blackness.

That's what he'd attempted to do. Disappear. But it was time to resurface. He'd known it, even before Josiah broached the subject weeks ago. New York shouldn't hold any dangers since Vittorio thought him dead. And Sarah would enjoy discovering the countryside. . . .

No. Bill clenched his jaw. He may be a "new man," as Josiah had told him, but marriage didn't fit in with his plans for a new life, either. Josiah would just have to understand.

Guilt swamped Bill. The missionary had done so much for him: opened his home and ministered to his needs both physical and spiritual, saved his life. Bill now looked forward to his nightly talks with Josiah and realized how heavily he relied on the man's insights and wisdom. His own father had never had time for him, never approved of him, and Josiah had filled the father role in Bill's life.

But marry Sarah? Asking him to link his life to another person's for all his natural-born days? Well, that was just asking too much.

&

Sarah sat on the floor of her aunt's hut. While Aunt Lefu prepared octopus for the evening meal, Sarah continued to weave the golden-white thin strands from the pandanus tree for the fine mat she had worked on for two years, as was custom for her dowry.

"The time has come that you should marry, Sarah. I do not understand your father in this matter of choice he's given you." Aunt Lefu raised her hands in irritation and shook her head of thick black hair. "I was told whom I would marry."

"But you were born to *taupo*. As a chief's daughter, more was expected of you."

Lefu's mouth thinned. "Your father's way will see you old and unmarried. Are there no boys in the village to interest you?"

Sarah wove the fronds. She didn't want a boy. She wanted a man. A man such as Bill.

Heat seared her cool cheeks, and Lefu's eyes narrowed.

"So, you have interest in a bridegroom! Is it Nua? He stares at you often with moon eyes."

Sarah ignored that. She didn't think much of Ono's young son, who exhibited as much intelligence as a land crab and proved to be about as agile.

Lefu grunted. "Very well. It is time we speak of what will be required of you."

Sarah briefly looked up, uncertain of what was coming.

"Your husband you must serve, and you must be submissive to him. But never let him see what lies within your heart. That shows weakness, Sarah. You must guard your emotions well, for that is your strength. I have taught you this since you were young, but still you forget. Do not be like the weak or simpering—like the silly women of this village, Meta and others. You are the granddaughter of a chieftain. Because of this, do not go with a suitor if he asks you on a nighttime tryst. You must show no eagerness, another failing you have. And it is not wise to walk around the island without a chaperone."

Sarah couldn't imagine always being guarded as many of the young, unmarried daughters of higher rank were. "I'm careful. I talk to no one."

"And what of this man Bill?"

Sarah's eyes snapped up from her task.

"You look at me in surprise. Did you think I would not learn of him and your walks over the island? Meta does not know how to control her tongue."

Sarah swallowed hard. "My father approves."

"Your father does not understand the ways of our people. If the village men thought you were violated, there might be no offers of marriage. It is bad enough you are a missionary's daughter. Do not add to those sins."

Uneasy, Sarah's glance went to the sun, lowering beyond the mountain. "It is late. I need to prepare the fish." At least, she hoped Bill and her father had caught fish. A second night of bananas, yams, and taro didn't appeal.

"Guard my words well, Sarah."

Her aunt's parting admonition followed Sarah the entire walk home. Bill approached her from the path to the beach, his face animated, so unlike the distance he'd shown since their return from the waterfall. Often these days she would catch him staring at her, but rarely did he speak.

"I caught a fish!" Bill announced. "With a spear!"

"That is good." Remembering her aunt's words, she tempered her happy smile at seeing him until her face was a mask of indifference. "I will go and prepare it. And you, Father?" She turned to watch as he came up behind Bill.

"Two small ones. His catch should adequately feed all of us. How is Lefu?"

"She is well." She hesitated. "She thinks it is time I seek a husband. Perhaps she is right." Without looking at Bill, Sarah walked to the hut to start a fire for the fish.

≈

Unable to relax, Bill took the path to the beach after his nightly talk with Josiah. His mind went to the meeting he'd had yesterday when several men had returned from their day of fishing, pulling their canoe up to the beach, and Josiah had made introductions.

A few of those men had been loudly teasing a skinny boy named Nua of his love for a young woman and a poem he'd written but never given her. Nua had cast quick glances to Josiah as he approached with Bill, as if nervous the older man should hear, and the others quieted upon seeing the missionary.

Surely such talk had not been a cause for shame. . .unless the reason for their sudden silence had to do with Sarah. Had she been the woman discussed?

She thinks it is time I seek a husband. Perhaps she is right.

Sarah's earlier parting words left an indelible imprint on Bill's brain. So what if Sarah married one of the villagers?

That certainly would solve his problem. If she gained interest in one of the island men, then Bill could depart to America in peace, freed from any guilt and matrimonial ties.

A woman's lilting laugh cornered his mind. Curious, he walked along the path to the beach, staying hidden beyond a fringe of palms.

Against the flame of sky that stretched over the waters, Sarah played with a boy and girl who'd wandered far from the village. They chased Sarah, all of them giggling, through the surf. Sarah visibly slowed her pace so they could catch her, and both children threw their arms around her waist, all three of them falling into the water, laughing harder. Pensive, Bill watched the gaiety a while longer before he turned and headed back up the path and into the hut.

Josiah sat at his desk and looked up from the letter he was writing.

"All right," Bill said without preamble. "I'll marry Sarah."

❧

Sarah stood and listened to the waterfall whisper to her one last time.

When Bill had approached her two nights ago and asked to speak to her alone, she wasn't prepared for the shock when he said her father wanted him to take her back with him to America on a ship that had recently arrived. But when Bill further explained that it would be to Sarah's benefit if she married him first, an arrangement to which her father also agreed, she'd only stared, speechless.

A loveless proposal for a marriage. An arrangement of convenience.

Her father later affirmed Bill's words, and they'd talked long into the night while Bill slept. She'd been curious about the world beyond her little island, and Father wanted her to learn of the customs and the land from which he came, though he'd assured her the decision to marry Bill would be hers alone. One day soon, according to Aunt Lefu, she must wed, and no villager attracted her as a potential bridegroom. As such, she'd thought she would spend her life serving her father, taking care of him, and that idea had been satisfactory.

Until Bill had washed up on shore.

"Sarah?"

She turned, startled to hear his voice. He appeared through the bushes.

"I thought I'd find you here. It's time. The ship leaves in an hour."

Nodding mutely, she kept her expression blank. She wouldn't let him know how terrified she was at this moment.

"Wait," he said before she could precede him onto the path.

She turned to look and felt the stem of a hibiscus slide into her hair above her ear.

"That's better. You should always wear flowers. They look good on you." His voice was as taut as his smile.

The next hour went by in a haze for Sarah. Standing beside Bill as her father read from the book he used for Christian ceremonies of this nature. . .her soft answers to his questions to love, honor, and obey mirroring the gravity of Bill's responses. . .the stiff kiss Bill imparted to her lips once her father pronounced them man and wife. . .the villagers' hugs and well wishes for a safe journey.

Only Aunt Lefu held herself aloof, distant from the others, though her parting hug to Sarah was warm. "I do not understand your choice, Sarah, or your wish to leave us. But I will always carry you in my heart. Remember all I have taught you."

"I will."

Her father hugged her long and hard, and she couldn't stem the tears that streamed down her cheeks.

"I shall miss you; I cannot imagine what life will be like without you." Sarah pulled back and memorized the lines of his dear, craggy face.

"I knew this day must come, long before you did." His own eyes were watery. "It's as it should be. Bill's a good man; he'll make you a fine husband." He put into her hands the cross on which he'd been whittling for weeks. Onto the wooden stick as long as her forearm and half its thickness, he'd carved beautiful wavy marks and pictures.

"It's a piece of our life. Each symbol represents a monumental event that took place, and each groove represents the love and prayers I continually have for you. The shape is in a cross to remind you that our Savior has been and always will be in control of your life and holds us together in spirit. Guard it well, Sarah."

Moved beyond words, she nodded, kissed his cheek, then turned to walk with her new husband toward the small ship that would carry her away to an indistinct world. Behind, the villagers lifted their voices in a song of farewell. Her hold on the cross tightened. Bleak uncertainty threatened her resolve not to cry.

Bill touched her arm. "It'll be all right."

She looked at him, then back at the ship, and continued her course.

six

Days later, Bill gripped the ship's rail. How much longer he could keep up this distance, he didn't know. Just to be with Sarah in close quarters, to smell her sweet fragrance, to look into her fathomless eyes, to hear the melody of her words was almost more than he could bear. And those times she inadvertently brushed against him sent fire surging through his veins. Purposely he stayed away, waiting until the early morning hours when he was physically exhausted and she was sound asleep before allowing himself to lie down, his back to her.

He'd half convinced himself that he married Sarah to repay the man who'd saved his life and in gratitude to Sarah for all she'd done—to help her find a good life in America as her father wished. Honorable intentions. All lies.

Now that he was being honest with himself, Bill knew his true reason for marrying Sarah was entirely selfish. He didn't want Sarah to come to him in submission; he wanted her to come to him in love. Nothing else would do.

He loved her and wanted her for his wife. She *was* his wife. And somehow, he would make her love a blackguard like himself. She'd only married him in compliance with her father's wishes. Bill had seen her daughterly obedience in every regard, and if she *did* have feelings for him, why then did she never show it? Her expression was always so placid. She'd rarely smiled since they married. The only time he'd seen Sarah display any emotion, besides her frolicking with the animals and children, was when she'd parted with her father. Then the tears had fallen in earnest, and he'd seen the

43

emptiness that hollowed her eyes.

Bill felt like a criminal, taking Sarah away from all she loved, even if it was at the request of her father. Somehow, he would get through these days at sea. Once they were in New York at his brother's home, the situation was bound to be easier than it was with them both being so confined.

At least the captain's orders made Bill's life a little easier.

☙

Her father's stories of what to expect couldn't prepare Sarah for life aboard a ship, especially one filled with sailors who spent their lives at sea. The shipping vessel on which they journeyed wasn't supplied with suitable quarters for a woman. However, when a few men showed immediate interest in Sarah within an hour after they'd boarded and set sail, and it almost led to a fistfight with Bill and the rowdy sailors, the captain informed them both that she and Bill would be given his quarters for the duration of the voyage. The captain asked Sarah to stay within the cabin to avoid further conflicts. She knew he wasn't pleased to have her aboard, being the superstitious sort who didn't cater to a woman being on his ship, but at both Bill's and her father's persuasion, he had allowed her passage.

The first few days, she'd been seasick and hadn't minded staying inside, but after a week, she recovered enough that if she didn't leave the cabin, she would go mad. Her father at some point had secreted his small Bible, filled with his handwritten notes, into the canvas bag containing all her worldly possessions from the island. And that thoughtful gift helped to fill many empty hours.

Bill, for the most part, stayed absent. In fact, he hadn't touched her since they'd boarded ship, and that confused her greatly. She knew little of what went on in a marriage; her aunt had left her ignorant in that regard. Perhaps he'd made no move toward her because he regretted taking her as his wife.

The torturing thought plagued Sarah's heart.

Nighttime had come, and the lure of fresh air, the need to leave such confining quarters, brought her out of the cabin. This late, it surely couldn't hurt to seize several minutes alone on deck.

She climbed the narrow stairs, alert to every sound and grateful for no sign of humanity. The salty air breezed across her face, and she inhaled a deep, cleansing breath before walking farther. To feel the coolness against her skin was sheer bliss after the imprisonment of the cabin. The sound of men's faint voices rolled from the front of the ship. She caught sight of Bill standing alone at the side.

Grabbing the rail, he looked out over the black water, where a shimmer of moonlight formed an obscure path. He stood as if a weight burdened his soul. All at once he straightened, turned.

"Sarah? What are you doing up here?"

Closing the distance, she noted he didn't seem pleased to see her. "No one is nearby. Why should I not be allowed to partake of fresh air as everyone else on board does? As you do?"

Her words made him flinch. "Those were the captain's orders, not mine."

Resigned, she gave a nod. "I will return."

"Wait." He blew out a breath. "A few more minutes won't hurt. And it *is* quiet."

She watched him, not understanding his odd behavior. One minute he seemed angry with her; the next, he coveted her company. All week, it had been like this.

He solemnly studied her face. His gaze went to her hair, and he gathered a thick strand of it. "Pretty Sarah. . .how it shines in the moonlight," he whispered. "Like rich black satin."

Stunned, Sarah didn't move, didn't speak. Bill continued to slowly rub the lock of hair between his fingers, staring at it as if he'd never seen it before, letting it fall bit by bit to her shoulder. When he returned his gaze to hers, she inhaled an inaudible, expectant breath at the intense look in his eyes, thinking he might kiss her.

Instead, he took in a deep lungful of air and let it out slowly through his mouth. "You should return to the cabin—before the captain sees us, and we're both in trouble."

"Will you come also?"

His glance toward her came quick, and she read surprise there before he averted his gaze to some point mid-deck.

"I'll be along later, long after you're asleep. Don't wait up." He turned his attention to the sea.

Now that he couldn't see her, Sarah allowed her mask of detachment to fall away at his rejection. Hurt drew her brows together, and the sting of tears came as she swiftly retraced her steps.

&

The crash of thunder awoke Sarah. Heart beating fast, she jumped to a sitting position, clutching the blanket. Another deafening crash made her whimper and recoil, hitting against Bill, who lay beside her. On the island, she'd hated the rainy season with its never-ending storms, but on a rocking ship, the sound seemed magnified. She felt vulnerable, alone, abandoned. Would they all die?

"Sarah?" Bill asked groggily. She felt him sit up. "What's wrong?"

She couldn't answer, couldn't stop trembling.

"Sarah?" His voice was curious, soft. "Is it the storm?"

She gave an abrupt nod, squeezing her eyes shut when a white flash lit the entire cabin and thunder seemed to crack against the side of the ship.

His arms closed around her, drawing her close. "Shhh, it's all right. This isn't so bad. I've seen worse. There's no reason to fear, pretty Sarah. The ship appears to be a seaworthy vessel."

He smoothed his hand over her hair, kissed her temple,

held her more tightly. His strength, his warmth helped to soothe her. She relaxed, resting her head against his shoulder. He stiffened.

"Don't let me go," she whispered, alarmed he might draw away.

And he didn't. All through the violent storm, he held her close to his heart. Even after the thunder abated, his arms remained around her. Now that the danger had passed, her senses became fully attuned to the man who held her. Her husband, and her mind wrapped around a night on the island. . .and a kiss.

Her heartbeat quickened, matching his.

"Sarah. . . ?"

His voice was hoarse, full of an emotion she couldn't discern, but one that had her lifting her face to his in entreaty. A flash of delayed lightning revealed his searching expression, but a flame kindled in his eyes, taking Sarah's breath away.

Their kiss was both tender and consuming. A give and take that shook Sarah to her core, while reassuring her heart that at last all would be well between them.

seven

New York was more than Sarah could have imagined and nothing close to what she had dreamed. Accustomed to life on her quiet island with only bird cries and the ocean's surf to sing to her, she was unprepared for the raucous dissonance of sound that was Manhattan.

Noisy automobiles chugged and roared and popped. Hordes of people walked the sidewalks, a far greater number than were in her village, and they spoke and shouted and laughed. Everywhere there was motion; everywhere confusion.

Unconsciously, she drew closer to Bill, clutching his sleeve, then scolded herself for doing so and released it. After that wondrous night they'd shared in one another's arms, Sarah had awoken to find Bill gone. Memory of her childish fear of the storm then broke through the cloud of sweet contentment and twined itself around her mind. She now regretted that she'd let him observe such weakness in her. Aunt Lefu would have been displeased. Sarah assumed that at some point later in the night, Bill had recalled her shortcomings, her panicked tears, her clutching tightly to him like a child, and had been disappointed in her weakness. No other explanation presented itself as to why he would leave her before daybreak and again put emotional distance between them—as he had put distance between them throughout the following weeks, though he'd been polite, even charming. She could not fault him for that. Yet after the intimacy they'd shared, he now seemed as if he were attempting to be a stranger.

Women dressed in boyish, drab dresses with their hair cut in bobs or piled in strange shapes on their heads and wearing outlandish hats, eyed Sarah with looks ranging from horror to curiosity to outrage. Sarah looked down at her sarong and unadorned loose hair. She did not fit in with these people.

Bill must have arrived at the same conclusion, for he immediately herded her to one of many similar buildings that lined the streets, putting her under the care of an elderly lady who hemmed and hawed throughout most of what she called a fitting. Within hours, Sarah was outfitted in a shapeless dress as drab as the rest of them she'd seen. She endured the changes for Bill, hoping he would then look at her with approval, hoping he would look at her at all.

He did look at her, but not in delight. Rather his eyes were sad. Trying to see what he did, she lowered her gaze to the calf-length, gray-checked chemise with its low waistline, and the thick braid hanging past her stomach that she'd allowed the lady to weave when Sarah would not let her pile it atop her head.

"We need to catch the train in an hour. Are you ready?" Bill's voice was somber, distant.

Sarah inwardly sighed. "Yes." Was she? If he did not accept her or approve of her appearance, how then did she expect his people to?

The huge expanse of Pennsylvania Station with its many levels of stairs overwhelmed Sarah. She did not resist clutching Bill's arm this time, fearing she might lose him in the crowds of people swarming all around her.

Only when they were safely sheltered within a compartment on a train did Sarah allow herself the pleasure of relaxing. She had never been on a train either, but she was so tired, and she closed her eyes.

❧

Bill watched Sarah as she slept. Her face lacked the color it had held on the island, her posture was weary, and Bill's heart constricted that he'd had to bow to the dictates of society and clothe her in a dress that seemed entirely inappropriate for his free-spirited Sarah. He'd been annoyed by the looks cast her way from snobbish women who'd crossed their path and had hoped to alleviate the problem with a portion of the money Josiah had given him for the journey. Yet the obnoxious ogling continued, and he knew Sarah must have felt their silent barbs. For himself, he didn't care. He'd had worse stares thrown his way. But for Sarah, he desired her happiness and comfort.

Since that night of heaven, when he and Sarah had become one, Bill had run the gamut of emotions. His love and desire to protect had intensified, but at the same time, when he'd awoken to see his beautiful Sarah lying beside him, oppressive anguish tore at his soul. Self-bitterness raged through him that he'd taken advantage of her vulnerability and allowed his own weakness, his strong desire to be with her, to overtake his objective.

Bill had never known love. Not from his parents, not from his associates, not from former girlfriends, of which there'd been a number. Yet those painted floozies with their selfish ambitions couldn't hold a candle to Sarah. For the first time, Bill knew what it was to love, and he desperately wanted her love in return.

Maybe if Sarah had told him she loved him after he'd whispered to her his own adoration as she lay within his arms, he'd feel differently. Maybe if she'd shown any emotion on her face the next morning when he'd bolstered enough courage to reenter their cabin. But she hadn't. Instead she regarded him, her face as placid as always, her eyes blank.

And that look had blasted his heart as surely as if she'd pulled the trigger of a gun.

Closing his eyes, he tried to rest. The next few hours of their uncertain future were trying enough without dredging up the recent past. That Brent would be surprised to see his long-lost brother was a given. Hopefully surprise would be the only negative reaction, and there would be a welcome. Bill had been given no opportunity to write a letter announcing their arrival, no method by which to send it, and even if he had, he didn't know the address of the reform school.

Reform school. He let out a derisive chuckle. For the past twelve years, he'd done his best to evade the police, and now he was bringing his new wife with him to a place that most likely contained bars on the windows.

But Vittorio was still out there, he and the rest of his mobsters. And until Bill was far away from Manhattan, he wouldn't feel safe. A small town near Ithaca seemed like the perfect solution.

≥∘

Once they exited the train, Sarah stood with Bill on the wooden platform. He carried her canvas bag and looked around the area, his features rigid. Clutching her father's cross to her heart for reassurance, she also studied the town. Here the buildings were much smaller, not so tall, and she counted only one automobile puttering along the street. A red- and white-striped pole stood nearby. On the window next to it, the words BARBER SHOP were painted in white.

Bill also stared in that direction and swept a hand over the back of his hair. "I guess if I want to make a good impression with my brother, I'd better get a trim. I let it grow good and wild on the island." He looked at Sarah, as if suddenly unsure what to do with her. "There's a shop you can visit next door. Why don't you wait for me there? A barber shop isn't a place for ladies."

Sarah nodded, taking comfort in the fact that he would be in the building beside her. This place was much quieter than the city in which the ship had docked, but she still felt in limbo in this strange new world.

They parted at the doorway. Sarah's heart went weak when

the expression in Bill's eyes softened for an instant, and he smiled. "I'll only be next door."

She watched as he disappeared into the barbershop. Her interest to explore revived, and she turned to see what this building contained. The room into which Sarah walked seemed dark after just coming out of bright sunlight. The area smelled of coffee and tobacco. Other scents tantalized— unusual but appealing scents—and she approached the wooden counter. An array of jars filled with mixtures of all shapes and colors heightened her curiosity.

"That horehound candy is especially nice, though I prefer fresh peaches and plums meself," a friendly but strange-sounding voice observed from behind her. The accent was unusual, unlike any Sarah had heard. She turned around to see a woman of about the same height as herself, with a flowered hat rakishly perched atop her piled-up hair. Her eyes, the color of indigo blue waters, sparkled with mischief and fun. Sarah felt a pang of homesickness as she was reminded of her father and his penchant for joviality. A baby lay nestled against the woman's shoulder.

The woman held out a hand. "Me name's Darcy. And you are?"

"Sarah." She could barely speak, for as the child yawned and opened his eyes, she saw the same turquoise blue as her husband's. A closer examination of the little round face made her catch a swift breath. This child could be her husband's! He looked like a small copy of Bill.

"Are you all right, luv?" Darcy asked in concern. Her dark brows raised in confusion, she looked at the golden-haired boy then at Sarah again.

Sarah strived for composure. "Yes. It's just that—"

The door suddenly opened, and in walked Bill. Sarah blinked. No, not Bill. This man wore different clothing, and he held a child of the same age. . .identical to the one the woman

Darcy held. The same in age and size, at least, though the child he held was a girl. Sarah looked back and forth between the two, then up into the man's face. The same turquoise-colored eyes, same long nose and high cheekbones. Only upon looking more intently could she tell his unshaven jaw wasn't quite as strong and defined as Bill's without his beard, his brows weren't as thick, his hair wasn't as long. Except for those small differences, they could be the same person.

Sarah swallowed and clutched the cross more tightly, feeling dizzy. For as she looked from face to face, she realized this must be her husband's family. Remembering snippets of conversation Bill had shared with her, she knew this must be the brother with whom Bill had been estranged for quite some time.

The door opened again. Bill stepped inside. "Barbershop's full. Too many people in line for me to wait around, and—" He cut off abruptly, halting his advance, as his image holding the child swung to face him.

Stunned silence crackled the air between them.

"Brent." Bill's word came out taut as he gave a slight nod.

"Bill. . ." The man holding the child blinked, then shook his head. "I don't believe it. Though the fact that you still exhibit a tendency for impatience doesn't surprise me in the slightest."

"Yeah, well, you know I never was one to bide my time well." Bill's words were casual, but Sarah could tell he was nervous. He looked at her, then moved her way. "And this is Sarah. My wife." His hand went to her back, and she was grateful for his support. Without it, she might have fallen in a dead faint. The blood seemed to surge from her head.

Bill's brother stared at her, his eyes wide in shock. After another set of tense seconds elapsed, Darcy glanced at him curiously, then stepped forward with a smile. "I knew the moment I laid eyes on you I'd like you, Sarah. You're an odd duck like meself, so we're a matched set. Welcome to the family." She gave her a quick one-armed embrace.

Sarah blinked. Bill stared. Brent gawked.

"Well now!" Darcy spoke again, her voice high and chipper as if to lighten the situation. She shifted the child to her other shoulder. "I think we should move this little reunion to Lyons' Refuge where it belongs. What d'ye say, guv'ner?" She looped her hand around Brent's forearm, moving closer to him.

He visibly relaxed, glanced at her, then back at Bill. "Before I agree, I feel it my duty to ask: Will we be expecting only the two of you? Or will the cops and robbers be beating a path to our door as well?"

Darcy laughed nervously. Sarah could see a bald little man had taken a stand behind the counter and listened with rapt attention. He slowly rubbed a cloth over some tins on a shelf, his widened eyes fixed on the group in front of him.

Bill's mouth quirked in a parody of a smile. "Well, little brother, I see you've found the quality of humor somewhere inside that intelligent brain of yours, after all." He softly snorted and gave a faint shake of his head as if in self-mockery. "And yes, it will be just the two of us."

Brent gave a curt nod. "In that case, you're welcome to visit. The wagon is outside. Come along, Darcy." He turned without waiting for Bill's reply.

Darcy gave an uncertain smile and followed. Sarah threw a sharp glance at Bill. His answering nod reassured, but now she wondered if these people would ever accept them as members of their household.

eight

That had not gone well.

Blowing out a heavy breath, Bill sat with Sarah in the back of the wagon that took them to Lyons' Refuge. All his plans to confidently approach Brent—clean-shaven, hair neatly trimmed, and clad in a decent suit of clothes—had failed. The shirt he wore was Josiah's, given to him after the remnants of his own shirt were thrown out. He had needed to wear it unbuttoned on the island since the man was slighter in build. But once they reached New York, Bill had forced the buttons through the holes, though the material strained across his shoulders and made movement difficult. And his trousers were frayed at the ends.

He supposed he should have purchased a suit of clothes while he waited on Sarah, but he didn't feel confident showing his face around the area on the chance someone might recognize him. On second thought, that chance was slim. A growth of beard covered his face, and his hair hung almost to his shoulders. He looked like what he was—a former castaway of a Pacific island. *Not* the impression he'd wanted to make on his brother as a man who'd renounced his corrupt behavior.

Sarah, on the other hand, looked wonderful. She may not completely have conformed to protocol concerning dress, but Bill wouldn't have her any other way. He loved her long hair and was glad she hadn't cut it in a bob or stuck it up in some ridiculous bouffant that some women seemed to favor nowadays. And those hats were absurd. His gaze went to the bobbing flower on top of Darcy's wide-brimmed number. He couldn't

55

say much for his sister-in-law's taste in clothing, but he liked the character she'd shown, more so when she made Sarah feel so welcome. And Brent was a father, too! Amazing. . .

Glimpses of the fair-headed twins on either side of Darcy's lap put a lump in his throat. For the first time in his life, Bill wondered what it would be like to be a father.

His gaze went to Sarah, and his heart lurched. She stared at him, anxiety in her eyes. He gave her a faint smile, but instead of responding, she looked down at her lap as though ashamed. Or disappointed. In him?

Bill flicked his eyes closed and averted his gaze to the back of the wagon and the rows of trees in full summer bloom on each side of the dirt lane. Somehow, he would capture her love and respect; there must be a way.

When the wagon reached Lyons' Refuge, as the sign outside the gate said, Bill stared in shock. No bars blocked the windows. No policemen strolled the grounds. What kind of place was this?

A large stone-and-wood house, simple and homey, stood on several acres of well-kept lawn. Beyond that stretched open land, and the only fences in evidence appeared to be those that kept livestock without and not criminals within. Bill spotted a few horses and cows. He could actually get to like it here. . . .

A chorus of boys' cries disrupted the peace as a small mob of miniature hooligans descended upon the wagon. Bill counted eight of them. Sarah's eyes widened.

"Master Brent, Master Brent," one of the smallest cried. "Herbert set a fire in the schoolroom and burneded the papers."

"Didn't mean to!" A redheaded, freckle-faced boy shot back. "It was an accident when I lit the stove."

"Unh-uh. You was mad."

"Boys!" Brent's roar silenced them. "That's better. We

shall discuss this further when we meet in an hour at the schoolroom, which I assume is still standing."

"Mr. Lyons put the fire out like this." The first boy clutched the wagon and stamped his foot up and down. "He had to stomp on it like an Injun."

"I am pleased to hear of the rescue of the schoolhouse, Jimmy. Now, you boys may resume your chores."

By this time, most of them had taken notice of Sarah and Bill in the back of the wagon. Their eyes grew so large that Bill could see the whites of them.

"Go on with you," Darcy said. "You heard Mr. Thomas."

They scattered like field mice.

Inside the large house, a second round of people, mostly adults, converged upon the newcomers. Bill felt overwhelmed; he could well imagine how Sarah must be feeling.

"Is there somewhere my wife could rest?" he asked in an aside to Charleigh Lyons, a plump redhead with a benevolent smile. "We've traveled a long way, and I know she's tired."

"Of course. Please, follow me," she replied with a British accent much like Darcy's.

She led them upstairs to a bedroom containing a four-poster bed. Bill's gaze traveled to the right and the horsehair sofa sitting alongside one wall.

"When we bought new furniture for the parlor, we brought that up here. I suppose one day we'll get rid of it, but for now this was the only place to store it and keep it safe from rowdy boys. Though my husband does have plans for building a storehouse soon."

A baby suddenly shrieked, then began bawling as if the world had ended.

"Oh, my. That's Clementine. I'm sorry." She turned to look at Sarah. "Please feel free to lie down. And welcome to our home."

Charleigh directed a quick smile to both of them before

bustling out of the room, leaving Bill alone with Sarah. She looked at him as if waiting for him to instruct her on what to do. He set her canvas bag on the sofa.

"I need to go speak with my brother. You should get some rest."

"They did not expect us. They do not know we intend to stay."

He winced at what he felt was quiet accusation. "There was no way to get a letter here from the island, and before I could find a telephone and get their number, we ran into them." He brushed his knuckles against her cheek. "Don't worry, pretty Sarah. I'll straighten it all out."

*

After he'd closed the door, Sarah put her hand to the cheek Bill had just touched. His unexpected caress had done more to soothe her turmoil than any words spoken.

Quietly, she moved toward the bed and lay upon it, still clutching her cross to her chest. The events of this day and the past weeks converged upon her, and she closed her eyes, squeezing away a tear. Homesick for her island, she tried to imagine her father's steady, quiet voice speaking to her on the morning of her wedding.

"Courage, my beautiful girl. All will be well. I'm convinced that God had this planned from the beginning."

She only wished she could believe it were so.

*

After they retreated to the study, Bill eased into the chair his brother motioned toward, unable to quench an ironic amusement. Once Bill had been the dapper young man in glad rags, dressed in expensive suits. Now Brent looked the well-dressed—if austere—gentleman, and Bill resembled a ragamuffin from the docks. He watched as Brent pulled some round spectacles from his pocket and slid them over his ears.

"Why are you here?" Brent came straight to the point.

Bill crossed his ankle over his leg, his wrists dangling over the chair arms with ease. "Ah, dear brother. You always did know how to make a man feel welcome." Brent's face reddened, and Bill's mocking smile slipped from his face. What was he doing? This was no way to earn sympathy. Nor did the usual sarcasm he'd shown Brent in the past feel like a secure fit anymore.

He sighed, wiped a hand over his beard. "My wife and I need a place to stay."

"A place to stay?"

"That's right. I'm not asking for charity; I'm good with my hands. I can take a gander at anything that needs fixing or building—"

Brent held up his hand, cutting his brother off. "We seem to be passing over a rather important issue in regard to our last meeting that took place at the train depot more than a year ago. If memory serves me correctly, you're a wanted man."

"The police aren't looking for me if that's what you're worried about. And neither is Vittorio." Too late, he wondered if he should have added the last. He had planned to tell him one day, yes, but after they'd settled in and the waters had smoothed over a bit.

"Vittorio?"

"The man I worked for. He thought it was curtains for me." Bill squirmed the slightest bit when Brent only stared. "He, uh, sent someone to rub me out."

"Rub you out? You mean he tried to kill you."

Bill's nod was short as he pulled up his shirt a fraction, showing the scar. "Knifed in the gut."

Brent stared at Bill's bronzed stomach with its white scar, then back into his eyes. "And you want to make your home here, and in so doing, bring imminent trouble upon the heads of all those staying at the refuge?" His words were incredulous.

"I told you. They think I'm dead. I was pushed overboard." Bill hesitated before saying the rest. "A dolphin saved me and took me to an island. Sarah found me and dragged me to the beach."

Brent's mouth dropped partly open, his stare one of speculative disbelief.

"I'm not making any of this up. I know it sounds farfetched, but it's the truth, so help me."

"You've been on this island this entire time?"

"Only for the past two months. I, uh. . ." The shirt Bill wore felt incredibly tight, and he shifted. "I recovered from my wound in the home of a missionary. Sarah's father." It was time to tell the rest, come what may. "Fact is, I found Christ there."

Brent's mouth dropped down farther, his eyes widening. "By Christ, I assume you mean—"

"Jesus Christ, God's Son." Bill gave a soft snort. "Is the concept so hard for you to believe? That your black-hearted brother can find salvation, too?"

Brent shook his head in wonder. "Well, it wasn't a burning bush, after all, but a dolphin."

"Excuse me?" Bill drew his brows together at his brother's faint remark.

"Never mind." Brent gave Bill the first real smile he had seen, though uncertainty tinged it. "I can't tell you how happy I am to hear that you changed your course in life. You have changed your course?" Brent added.

"I wouldn't be here if I hadn't. I figured a place that gives young criminals a second chance might be willing to give an old criminal one, too." His words came sincerely from a heart that he now laid bare before his brother. "I'm not happy about the past, Brent. If I could turn back the clock, I would, and I'd do things differently. But I can't. So I'll just have to muddle through somehow and hope something right comes of it."

"We all have that problem, wishing we'd done things differently. Yet God can steer you in the right direction if you ask Him."

"I have."

Brent stared at his clasped hands a taut moment, then rose from the chair. "I'll have to take this up with the board. I don't have the authority to make such weighty decisions without approval."

"That's all I ask." Bill stood, considered, then held out his hand.

Brent started, obviously taken aback, but reached across the desk and accepted Bill's hand in a shake. They stood that way for a moment, tears welling in their eyes.

It was the first physical contact the two brothers had shared since Bill ran away from home twelve years ago.

nine

Sarah often felt adrift in an ocean whose wild waves splashed all around her. Since Stewart Lyons and the rest of the board had approved her and Bill living at the refuge, life had taken on a surreal quality. On the island, she had pored endless hours through her father's many books, greedily soaking up every word about the world far from which she lived. But nothing could have prepared her for life at Lyons' Refuge.

Fifteen boisterous boys made their home there, ranging in ages from six to sixteen. All of them formerly in trouble with the law, they had been sent or brought to the refuge by Stewart Lyons, the headmaster of the reform school. Among those helping him with the massive task of improving the boys' minds and hearts was his wife, Charleigh.

Charleigh and Darcy, the cook, were an entity unto themselves. Full of fun and wit, Darcy thought nothing of speaking her mind, surprising Sarah, who'd always been taught restraint. It amazed Sarah to learn that both women had met in a London jail cell. She listened with rapt attention to their personal stories and to how they founded the school when Stewart, a former attorney, had built the place while Charleigh served her sentence in London.

Always quiet, Sarah didn't mind sitting on the fringes of the women's conversations, absorbing all they said. Yet one afternoon, as the women discussed the daily details of the household, Sarah spoke.

"What can I do for the refuge? I want to help, as well."

Both women looked at her, taken aback by her sudden

entry into the conversation.

"I could always use help in the kitchen," Darcy said. "Since Irma moved away to her sister's, I'm the only cook here now."

"Can you cook?" Charleigh's eyes were kind.

"Yes. I know how to prepare fish, octopus, eel. . ." Sarah ended her list when the women gave her blank stares. She looked down. "But not the food you have here in America, no."

"Say. . ." Darcy's voice sparkled. "I have an idea, but I'll need to speak with Brent first. Have you ever taught children?"

"In the village, I helped my father with his missionary efforts."

"How lovely. Would you be willin' to speak with the boys about life on your island? It might do them a world of good, opening up their minds to new adventures and the like. Let them see how the other part of the world lives. They certainly seemed to like that book *Robinson Crusoe*."

"I agree," Charleigh said. "That's a splendid idea, Darcy."

Sarah willed her heart to stop beating so fast. Teach a roomful of fifteen boys, some of them young men? The children she'd ministered to had been small. She kept her face a mask and nodded. "If my husband approves, I can do this."

"Wonderful. I'll speak with Brent tonight."

Feeling suddenly unable to breathe, wondering if she'd spoken too soon, Sarah excused herself and went outside. She strolled along the grounds, taking in the scenery.

Here in New York the trees didn't have fronds or fruit and coconuts growing from within their boughs as they did on the island. These trees were covered in a mixture of greens, from light to dark, with smaller leaves of serrated or round shapes, different from the palms. But they stood taller and gave much shade. And though here the air was cooler than the sultry heat of her island at noonday, the shade was welcome since the sun shone brightly.

In the distance she could see Bill on a ladder as he stood near the roof of the barn and pounded with a hammer. She drew closer.

His shirt and hair were damp from perspiration. After a time, he stopped, as though sensing her silent presence, and looked over his shoulder. He no longer wore a beard, though he'd kept a faint mustache and had trimmed his hair. The effect was pleasing but made him seem different from the man she'd learned to know on the island. It almost seemed as if he had wrought the physical changes to underscore the distance that remained between them.

"Sarah. Is everything all right?"

"I would like to speak with you if I may."

Bill glanced at the roof, as if he'd really rather pound on it some more, then looked back at her and gave a swift nod. He climbed down the ladder and faced her.

"Okay. You've got my undivided attention."

As he had hers. She could feel his warmth, his nearness, and something went weak inside her. His blue eyes were piercing, though they contained gentleness and not anger, touching her very soul. With a sad little inward sigh, she wondered what had gone wrong between them, so much so that he no longer wanted her.

She told him about Charleigh and Darcy's proposal, and he smiled. "That sounds like a great idea."

"You approve?"

"Of course. I think it might be good for you, Sarah. You have such circles under your eyes lately." He gently brushed his fingertip underneath her eye as he spoke, so lightly, it almost wasn't a touch at all.

Yet Sarah felt the caress down to her very soul. She held her breath.

"But are you sure you can handle the task?" He lowered his

hand to his side. "I realize it's been difficult for you to learn a new manner of living, and this place isn't your usual sort. I know you've been homesick."

Sarah swallowed back the emotion that rose to her throat. Missing her father and the island had been expected. Missing her husband's touch and presence had not.

"I believe I can do this."

"Then you should." He looked at her seconds longer, then glanced away. "I have to get back to work. That roof needs repairing before any more rain falls."

Sarah didn't want to go. "Is there anything I can do to help, Bill? Perhaps you would like a glass of water?" She wished she'd thought to bring some with her.

"That would be swell."

"Swell?" A vision of water ballooning into a huge bubble formed in her mind.

He grinned. "Meaning I'd like some very much, thanks. I think it's time I teach you slang, though Brent would have a conniption. He's very proper, in case you hadn't noticed." He winked slightly as if sharing a joke.

Again her heart felt as though it no longer belonged to her. The thought of spending time with her husband in any capacity birthed new hope within. "I should like to learn this slang if it would please you." *I should like to learn everything there is to know about you,* she silently added.

He looked at her a long moment. His smile faded, and a tender expression entered his eyes, reminding her of that long-ago night.

"Sarah?"

"Yes, Bill?"

"Let's skip out on the noonday meal and go have ourselves a picnic. There's a lake not too far from here, I'm told. We could go there."

His words slowly brought to life a part of her that had started to die.

ి

Excited at the prospect of spending time alone with his wife in the pleasurable atmosphere of a picnic, Bill hurried through his task of fixing the roof. When he entered the main house, however, Sarah was nowhere to be found.

"I believe she went upstairs to lie down," Charleigh offered as she set one of the two dining-room tables. "She wasn't feeling well, poor thing."

Worried, Bill took the stairs by twos. "Sarah?" he asked as he opened their bedroom door.

She lay upon the bed, still. Her eyes remained closed.

He hurried to the bedside and knelt down, putting a gentle hand to her shoulder. "Sarah, are you all right?"

Her eyes opened. "Bill?" she asked, as though coming out of a fog. Her eyes grew more alert. "Is it time for our picnic?"

"Never mind about that." He gently pushed her back down when she started to rise. "We can do it another day. You look tired, and maybe you should just rest this afternoon." He didn't like how pale her face appeared, and her mouth seemed strained.

"I would like to go with you on this picnic."

"Another time, Sarah. This whole journey to America has taken quite a toll on you. You've hardly had any rest since we got here. Not that I've seen, anyway." He attempted a smile, though concern pounded through his brain. "Your father wouldn't be at all happy with me if I didn't take the best care of you. I promised him I would, and I don't intend to let him down." By referring to her father, he hoped she would see reason, since she respected the man so.

Sarah's eyes grew sad for an instant, before the emotionless mask again slipped into place. Bill scolded himself for an unwise decision. Broaching the subject of her father had only served to increase her loneliness and homesickness.

"Very well, Bill. I will do as you wish." She turned from him, curling up on her side.

He stood looking down at her forlorn form for the longest time, strongly wanting to lie down beside her, to take her in his arms and comfort her.

Instead, he turned and left the room.

ten

Sarah heard the door close. Only then did she open her eyes. Heaviness threatened to weigh her spirit down, and she felt like she might retch. Bill had so quickly found an excuse to cancel their picnic, as if he'd regretted his impulsive invitation. His comment about her father had merely served to emphasize what she already knew. Bill married her at her father's request, to please him. Perhaps in gratitude for saving Bill's life.

Again, she asked herself the question she'd posed since the first night on the ship: Was there hope for their marriage? If only she had someone to confide in, someone who could point out to her what she was doing wrong. She loved Bill, if love meant that every ounce of who she was desired to be with him, to know him, to share in his every success, and to comfort him in his defeats. If only Aunt Lefu were here to guide her and give her advice She tried to show strength and not weakness, but as her aunt had often scolded her, she still had much to learn. Too often, Sarah revealed what lay enclosed within her heart. Through her eyes, which her father told her were a mirror to her soul. And through her expressions that she knew were the windows of her emotions. Perhaps the fact that her father was the type of man to exhibit his feelings made it more difficult for Sarah not to do the same.

With a sigh, Sarah rose to a sitting position and swung her feet to the floor. She still felt dizzy but desired no further sleep. Her gaze went to the cross on the bed-stand table, and she reached for it. Gently she ran her fingers over the grooves and the wavy lines in the smooth wood.

"Pray for me, Father. For both of us. Bill and I are in great need of your prayers."

Though she had looked at the cross many times, she had never actually studied it. Now her gaze went to the symbol carved at the top. A sun and moon, with the crescent of the moon inside the sun. From conversations with her father, she knew what that meant. The sun was her father, the moon her mother. The two were combined to show unity. Their marriage.

She looked at the next symbol, lower down, a crown next to the same sun bearing the moon, and smiled. Her father had once told her that her name meant *princess*. A fitting choice, since her grandfather had been a chieftain, but perhaps there was more to it than that. She pondered the thought, then looked still lower.

Here the crown lay next to a waterfall, with the sun-moon in the background hovering over it. Her mother and father protectively watching over her as a child while she played near her favorite spot, no doubt. She pressed her fingertips atop the symbol, memories of happier times swimming to her mind. After a while, she looked down at the next symbol.

A weaker sun had been carved to the left and a heavy line separated it from the crescent moon, which had a tiny moon inside it. Tears welled in Sarah's eyes. The death of her mother and stillborn child. A girl, her father once told her.

Unable to complete her study of the cross, Sarah brought it to her heart and held it there.

❧

Disappointed about the canceled picnic, Bill didn't feel like joining the throng at the dinner table and instead slipped into the kitchen to grab a sandwich. Darcy stood at the counter, humming and slicing bread, which she piled onto a platter.

"Mind if I help myself?" Bill motioned to the bread.

"You're not eating with the rest of us?"

"Not much up to it. Thought I'd just grab a bite in here and then head back to work." He eyed the platter of sliced roast beef. "Mind if I have some of that, too?"

"Help yourself. Is Sarah not coming down either?"

"She wasn't feeling well." He studied Darcy's kind eyes that never seemed to snub anyone. "Would you mind too much going up and looking in on her after the meal? I think she's homesick, and a women's chat-to-chat might perk her up."

"Sure thing, guv. I'm always ready for a friendly chat."

She offered him a smile, allowing him to fork hefty amounts of roast beef on his bread before she grabbed the two platters and left the kitchen. Bill pumped water into a glass, then headed for the small table in the corner. Before he could take a bite, Brent strode into the room.

"It has come to my attention that you plan to dine in the kitchen instead of partaking of the meal with the rest of us."

Bill gave a curt nod.

"May I ask why?"

"I just don't feel up to all the lively chatter right now." Bill hoped he would get the point.

Instead, Brent pulled a chair out and sat down across from him. "You never were the type of man to be labeled as an introvert. Is there a problem?"

Bill stared at the sandwich he held before lowering it to his plate. It might help to get it off his chest, and Brent was his brother. What a switch, though! Bill had always been the one to steer Brent when they were boys, and he'd never thought of him as anything but a kid brother, someone who needed to be taught, not a teacher. Yet Brent was a teacher, come to think of it, and a good one according to what Bill had heard.

"It's about me and Sarah." And with that opening line, the entire story of their meeting on the island up through the arranged marriage came gushing forth. However, he didn't tell Brent about the one night he had shared with Sarah on the ship; that was too personal, too special.

Brent removed his spectacles and polished them. Bill relied on every store of patience he possessed as he waited.

"One tidbit of information I've learned throughout my courtship and marriage to Darcy is the importance of acting upon how you feel. If you love your wife, do not only tell her so, but show it in your actions." Brent replaced his spectacles over his ears.

Tell her? Bill shied from the idea, picturing Sarah's bland, expressionless reaction. He couldn't take that again. "Exactly how do you recommend I show her? I've tried by dressing her like the other women so she wouldn't feel like an outsider. I've tried by suggesting a picnic, though we have yet to go on it. I've tried by giving her time alone to adjust to this new life."

"Those things are all well and good, but I meant to show her in a more personal manner. A poem, a touch, a kiss." Brent reddened. "Surely I don't need to go into detail. I know you were quite the ladies' man. Women like romance. Be a romantic, but most importantly be considerate of her feelings and put her best interests before your own."

Bill wondered how Sarah would respond to such overtures. With acceptance and joy, or with no expression whatsoever? He sighed, then directed his thoughts to his brother. "You've changed a lot in fourteen months. There was a day when you would never speak so openly about personal matters."

"Being married to Darcy does that to a person." Brent smiled. "I fear her spontaneity and proclivity to speak her mind have rubbed off on me somewhat."

"There you go with those big fancy words again," Bill mocked, more in amusement than ridicule. "You know, I used to envy you all your knowledge and your ability to make something worthwhile of yourself. Someone people could look up to and admire."

Brent's face went slack in shock, and his mouth fell open. "You admired me?"

"Still do."

"I always assumed you thought little of me."

Bill could understand why, recalling past unkind remarks to Brent. "I think part of why I talked the way I did had to do with your Christianity. I didn't understand it, and in a bizarre way that you probably wouldn't understand, it threatened me. My words to you were more of a defense, but yeah, Brent, I've always thought you were quite a whiz, the best brother a guy could have. You always had the smarts up here." Bill tapped the side of his head. "Ever since we were kids."

Brent removed his spectacles, foggy with what looked suspiciously like tears, and cleared his throat. "In those days, I thought you were a really swell guy, too."

Bill stared, this time the one to let his mouth hang open.

Brent chuckled. "Surely you must realize that, being a schoolmaster to fifteen boys from all walks of life, I've heard my share of slang."

"Well, yeah, I know you've heard it. But I never thought I'd hear you say it."

Polishing the mist from his spectacles, Brent again replaced them on his head and leveled a steady look at Bill. "Should you make mention of the fact, I will aggressively deny it. After all, I have a reputation as a stuffy schoolmaster to uphold." His light tone belied his grim words.

Bill chuckled, liking this change in his brother. Mentally, he took off his hat to Darcy, certain her love had been the needed factor to get Brent to lose some of his somberness.

Brent rose from the table. "Now, why don't you come and join the rest of the family for luncheon? Unless you truly would prefer to eat your sandwich in here?"

The invitation and inclusion of Bill in the word *family* had been the first sign of acceptance on Brent's part since Bill arrived at the refuge almost a week ago.

Feeling hopeful again, Bill nodded. "Thanks. Maybe I will join you guys after all."

He walked around the table to his brother, warmly clapping a hand to his shoulder for an instant, and followed Brent to one of the dining tables.

Fifteen hungry, impatient, lively boys waited. Bill noticed his chair wasn't the only one vacant.

"Where's Darcy?" Brent asked, taking his chair.

"She went up to take a plate to Sarah." Charleigh tied a napkin around her small daughter's chin. Clementine sat in a highchair, banging on the table with her palm, as if picking up on the boys' impatience. "Hush, Clemmie, that's no way to act."

"She's been gone for ages," Joel, a blond scamp said. "I think she musta got lost."

"I'm sure she wouldn't mind if we began the meal without her." Charleigh took the plump hand of her little girl and of the boy to her right. Her husband, Stewart, sitting at the opposite end of the table, did the same to the boys on either side of him. Bill likewise took the hands of the little boys put on either side of him, reaching across Sarah's empty chair to take Joel's hand. The older boys at the other table did the same. As they all said grace, Bill wondered about Sarah, and silently added a prayer that God would help her. Help both of them.

eleven

Sarah bent over the chamber pot in misery. She heard a light knock on the door, but before she could answer, her stomach released its contents again. She was barely aware of anyone entering the room.

"Oh, my." Darcy's voice oozed compassion as the woman knelt beside Sarah and laid her palm against her back. "You poor lamb."

Spent, Sarah crawled back on her hands and knees and sat against the wall for support. She closed her eyes and heard Darcy rise. The clink of the pitcher and water pouring into the basin filled the quiet, and she sensed Darcy in front of her again. A cool, wet cloth was pressed to her forehead.

"Thank you." Sarah opened her eyes.

Darcy regarded her, sympathy etched on her face. "Have you been this way long, luv?"

"Three days. I cannot remember being sick a day in my life. The journey must have been too taxing, as Bill said. These past weeks, I've also been dizzy at times and must need more rest."

"In this matter, I think Bill is wrong. Not about the rest though."

She looked at Darcy in confusion, noticing the light dancing in her eyes.

"Sarah." Darcy pressed her hand against Sarah's forearm, her action eager. "Unless I miss me guess—and I don't think I do since I've seen the same before in Charleigh and meself—you are with child!"

Sarah blinked, stunned by the words, though they rang true

through her mind and settled deep within her heart. She had always been regular with her cycles and assumed the stressful journey had delayed it. A baby. . .Bill's baby.

A wondering smile lifted her lips. "A baby."

Darcy chuckled. "Seems to me you've recovered somewhat. I doubt you'd want the meal I brought up for you, so I'll just take it away, shall I?"

A stab of fear tore through the gilded dream, and Sarah grabbed Darcy's arm. "What will I do? I know nothing of being a mother. I've helped to bring a child into the world in the village of my mother's people, but that is all. I had no mother to teach me, and my aunt did not speak of such things."

Darcy patted her hand. "You'll do fine. Something is inborn in a woman that God put there. I can't explain it meself, but when the time comes that the babe is laid in your arms, you'll know what to do. And I had twins my first experience!" She laughed.

Even physically exhausted, Sarah caught onto Darcy's words. "Your first. . ."

Darcy nodded, her grin widening. "Aye, luv. I be in the same position as you. So what say we help one another and support each other when our times arrive?"

Sarah felt reassured in knowing that they shared this bond. Another thought invaded, making her tremble.

"Sarah?" Darcy's brows pulled together in worry.

"Don't tell Bill. He must not know."

Darcy's eyes widened in incredulous surprise. "And how do you plan on keepin' it from him? When your stomach starts balloonin' out, he'll be bound to wonder."

Sarah averted her gaze, sliding her teeth over the edge of her upper lip. "There has been. . .difficulty between us."

"News of a babe coming into the world might help matters," Darcy softly suggested.

Or they might make things worse, and Bill might turn completely away from her.

"Please, Darcy. I will tell Bill when I feel it is the proper time."

"It's not me place to give such news to your husband, luv. Only Sarah, a word of caution. Charleigh did the same with Stewart, and I know she'll not mind me tellin' you, but it caused nothin' but pain for the both of them. What she feared wasn't true, and they could have both been saved a great deal of worryin' if she'd been up front about it. Don't wait too long."

Sarah closed her eyes, knowing Darcy was right, but at the same time, fearing she might be wrong.

❧

To Bill, Sunday morning at Lyons' Refuge could best be described as well-ordered chaos. The entire household was swept into a whirlwind as Stewart, Charleigh, Brent, and Darcy rounded up all fifteen boys, saw to it they were clean and in their best clothes, fed them, hurried them, and then herded them into two Tin Lizzies and one horse-driven wagon for the mile-long ride to church.

Lyons' Refuge was a complete anomaly to Bill. He chuckled to himself at how quickly he'd picked up on Brent's vocabulary to think of such a word. Little like a reformatory and more like a boys' school, the motto at the refuge was: "Love tempered with discipline." Bill saw evidence of that every day. Stewart and Charleigh, Brent and Darcy, never failed to listen to the young scamps, never failed to give a needed hug, but at the same time they meted out any deserved discipline. The punishment always fit the crime yet was constructive.

When Clint wrote on the barnyard wall words and pictures of a crass nature, he was given the disciplinary action of painting the entire barn. Last evening after two boys, Joel and Herbert, got into a fight, they were made to sit on the same stair step and told they must remain there and would not receive supper until they worked out their differences in a mature fashion. When everyone gathered around the tables, Bill noticed the two boys were there, joshing each other and laughing, obviously the best of friends again.

Sarah came downstairs. Bill pushed away further musings of the refuge and approached his wife. "Are you feeling better today?"

"Yes, Bill. Thank you." Her smile was faint. "I look forward to visiting an American church."

"Well, then. . ." He slipped his arm through hers. "Let's not keep the others waiting." She seemed improved, though he detected her slight trembling. "Did you eat breakfast?"

She seemed to blanch. "I had a muffin and some berries. It was all I wanted."

Bill didn't argue, but he didn't like the fact that her appetite had diminished since they'd arrived in New York. The thought again brought guilt, since he knew her condition stemmed from her missing her father and her island.

Angry with himself, though he'd only done what her father wanted by bringing Sarah to America, he gave a stiff nod and escorted her to one of the automobiles.

At the little white church, the members of the refuge filled up three entire pews. Bill listened to the minister preach about deceit and was reminded of Josiah in that the preacher had the same quiet fervor as the missionary. Sarah, too, sat alert beside Bill, her attention riveted to the pastor, whether it was because of the message or the likeness to her father, Bill wondered.

After the service, many came forward to greet the new-comers to Lyons' Refuge. Bill was maddened at the haughty stares from two old crones directed to Sarah from across the room, likely because of her desire to wear her hair in one long braid and keep it uncovered. Or perhaps the women's censure stemmed from the fact that Sarah was half Polynesian.

He glared at the women who had the effrontery to think themselves superior to his wife and was satisfied when they grew flustered and averted their attention. No doubt they'd heard about Brent's murdering mobster brother and feared what he might do to them. Not that Bill would hurt any woman, then or now. But it satisfied him to know he'd made an impact, which he hoped would mean an end to further hostilities directed toward Sarah. She seemed not to notice, but then her expression rarely gave away her feelings.

The pastor welcomed both Bill and Sarah with sincere warmth, and shook Bill's hand with gusto. "I'm Pastor Wilkins. I've heard so much about you."

"I'm afraid to ask what, though I can imagine. Let me just state from the start, I'm not the same man I was."

"I'm relieved to know it." The pastor's eyes sparkled.

"And this is my wife, Sarah."

"Hello, Sarah." His smile was genuine. "It's a pleasure to have you and your husband join our little community. You must meet my wife. She loves stories of adventure, and I'm certain she'd enjoy hearing about your island."

Bill looked around expectantly.

"Sadly, she's not here today. Her mother took ill, and she's gone to visit her."

"I'm sorry to hear that." Sarah looked at Bill, then back to the pastor. "May I ask a question?"

"Certainly."

"You spoke of Moses and Aaron and the golden calf. I have never heard this story. My father spoke mainly of the teachings in the New Testament. Is it truly a sin to pay homage to other gods? If one worships Jehovah as the main God, is it wrong to visit the temples of other idols?"

Astounded at Sarah's forthrightness, Bill realized she must have been accustomed to approaching her father with spiritual questions. The pastor didn't seem one bit fazed by her candor, though a woman within hearing distance turned to look sharply at her, caught sight of Bill, and looked away again.

"My first question to one who does these things is why visit the temples?"

"Where I come from, the bond of family is strong."

"So it is to please family?"

"In part. Also the curiosity to know and understand."

"I see." The pastor's expression became grave. He looked up, seeming to just notice they were drawing unwanted attention from a few women who had edged closer, though they appeared to be in quiet conversation with one another.

He shook his head with an expression of frustrated tolerance, then returned his gaze to Sarah. "I should like to talk with you on this matter further. I'm sorry to say, this is not the time to do so. Perhaps later this week you can come by for a visit? I live in the brown house, farther down the road. My wife should have returned by Wednesday."

Sarah looked up at Bill. He nodded. "I'll drive her here myself."

✪

The changes that took over her body confused and amazed Sarah but also stressed to her the truth of the matter. She was indeed with child. Most confusing to her was her wide range of emotions and how she could travel from joy and smiles to despair and tears within moments. Since the day they'd arrived at the refuge, every night Bill remained downstairs long after the household went to sleep. When he did come up, he slept on the sofa, though it looked uncomfortable despite the blanket he'd thrown over it. He had not touched Sarah or shared her bed since that night on the ship, and because of this, Sarah was able to hide her condition from him. When her stomach became queasy, it was an easy matter to slip from the room as Bill lay sleeping far on the other side, against the wall.

Tonight as she quickly padded to the door, Bill stirred and rolled over onto his back. "Sarah?"

Her heart jumped, and she willed it to be still. "I'm fine. I will be back in a moment." Quickly she hurried out before he could stop her, afraid she would not make it in time. When she returned, shaky but relieved, Bill again lay sound asleep. Light snores whispered past his lips.

The moon washed through the window, spilling onto the sofa. She went to stand before him, admiring his handsome face, which looked so like a little boy's in slumber. No worry lines or tension marred his features in sleep. Unable to resist, she braced her hand against the sofa arm and bent to brush her fingertips against his smooth cheek.

Would their son look like Bill?

Would Bill welcome a child into his life?

A swift rush of fearful uncertainty made her draw her hand away and return to her lonely bed. Their own troubles aside, Sarah knew Bill despised his father and had run away from home to escape the man's severity. According to Bill, his father had loathed and ridiculed him, and his mother had shown no love either. Both brothers endured a childhood of sorrows, and Sarah wondered if Bill might now resent the babe that lay within her belly. Resent her for carrying this child.

Torn by the thought, Sarah clutched the pillow and squeezed her eyes shut to try to thwart the hot tears that threatened. However could she bear it if Bill came to despise her? His apathy was hard enough to endure, though at times he exhibited politeness or even gentle regard. Yet he acted nothing like he did on the island or during that one incredible night on the ship.

Sarah curled on her side into a ball, fearful she had already lost him and not understanding the reason for it. If he did turn completely away from her, her heart would surely wither and die.

twelve

Bill awoke from a dream, heart beating fast. Chased by Vittorio's mobsters, he'd been cornered and had looked down the barrels of eighteen guns before their silent explosions shook him from sleep. He swallowed hard, wiping the sweat from his face. A woman's muffled sobs startled him.

Sarah?

He sat up and looked toward the four-poster. In the moon's glow, he could see that she lay on her stomach, her face buried in the pillow, shoulders shaking. Grief tore through his heart to witness her pain. Would this intense homesickness ever subside or, better yet, depart from her?

He didn't stop to consider his actions. His wife, who rarely showed emotion, was hurting deeply. Even if it was in part due to his action of bringing her here, Bill could not resist going to her. Approaching the bed, he felt a tug pull at his heart at how forlorn she looked among the expanse of white sheeting.

He settled himself beside her and laid his hand on her back. "Sarah?"

She stiffened, tried to capture her sobs.

The pain in Bill intensified. *No, Sarah, no. Don't pull away from me again. Don't retreat behind a mask of indifference, even if it's all you feel toward me. Even if you can't bring yourself to love me as I love you.* These words he whispered in his heart; he didn't dare air them aloud when he knew that to do so might again give her the power to wound him if she could not or would not reassure him his fears were in vain. If she didn't respond.

He moved closer and gathered her into his arms. Thankfully, she didn't resist.

Another torrent of tears soaked his nightshirt, which she clutched in one small hand. Closing his eyes, he held her tightly until the moon shifted and white light covered the counterpane. Even after she cried herself to sleep, Bill didn't let go. Enjoying the feel of his wife in his arms, he also closed his eyes and slept.

❧

Sarah awoke with the sense of something being different. Curious, she opened her eyes. She lay alone in her bed; a glance around the room showed Bill wasn't anywhere in sight. Then she remembered. He had been there with her. He had held her the entire time she cried, and that was the last she remembered.

Heat suffused her face. Her aunt Lefu would have been appalled to learn of Sarah's weakness. "Never let your husband see you cry," she had told Sarah one day. "It is a grave mistake, for then he will look upon you with contempt." Though Sarah noticed not all of her aunt's admonishments related to the way other village women acted, Aunt Lefu was highly respected by her husband and by all those in the village. She was a strong woman.

For a moment, Sarah allowed herself to treasure the memory of being held against Bill's warmth, feeling protected, his arms firmly around her. She sighed, wondering if he had pitied her weakness and that was why he'd come to her. Yet pity was just as bad as contempt. Sarah desperately wanted Bill's respect, for him to think of her as strong. And she wanted his love.

With a hopeless sigh, she pulled off the voluminous bed gown Charleigh had given her. Before dressing, she laid a hand against her bare stomach, thinking of the life inside her. Soon this child would grow, and her stomach would expand. She would have to tell Bill, but she could not bring herself to do so yet. She must find clothes to hide her condition.

While she made her own sarongs on the island, she wasn't familiar with the fashion of this drab-colored American dress that hung so slack, making her form almost boyish. Yet that was how Bill wanted her, so that is how she would be. She desperately wished to please her husband. It wasn't so much a matter of subservience, though Sarah had been taught that, but the desire to do all she could to make Bill happy.

Deciding she would speak to Darcy, Sarah washed her face of the dried tearstains, dressed, and went downstairs. As she reached the foyer, Bill walked in from the parlor.

They both stopped, staring at one another.

Smoothing her expression into blandness, Sarah waited. A barrage of thoughts volleyed against her mind. Pleasure at the memory of being held in his arms; fear that he now thought her weak and pitied her, or worse still, regarded her with contempt; apprehension at the somber look on his face. His eyes that she had thought gleamed upon seeing her now looked shuttered, closing her out.

"Good morning, Sarah. You're feeling better today I trust?"

His cold, polite words struck her as surely as if he'd slapped her. She struggled to maintain her placid expression. "Yes, thank you. I feel as if I could eat breakfast."

"I'm glad to hear it." He looked at her a moment longer, then gave a tight nod and left.

At the click of the front door, all Sarah's resolve to remain strong threatened to lift from her heart. But she firmed her shoulders and headed for the kitchen, while within, her world crumbled down around her feet.

❧

Bill stared across the grounds, idly watching the boys do their chores. He had hoped that things would be different between them after last night. But again, Sarah had shunned him with her cool regard, blasted him with another of her well-aimed bullets to his seeking heart. If there had been the slightest flicker of expression on her face, the slightest amount of joy upon seeing him. . .

He closed his eyes and swallowed hard. He would earn Sarah's respect and love or die trying. He'd never treated her like other women he'd known—except for that one predatory kiss on the island that shamed him to this day—and he had no idea how to gain her love. His hopeless thoughts moved into a hopeful prayer, and that brought the memory of the pastor's invitation three days ago.

Today he would take her to see Pastor Wilkins, to talk with him and his wife. They needed time alone, away from the constant chaos of the refuge. Always someone stood nearby or walked into the room, interrupting them whenever he did try to talk with Sarah. Maybe he'd even take her on that promised picnic. Show her that hidden spot by the lake, which he'd found last week and knew she would enjoy. Sarah had said she was feeling better today, even talked about eating a meal.

He would talk to Darcy, ask her to pack them a lunch, and surprise Sarah with his plan.

❧

"What's botherin' you, luv?" Darcy asked as Sarah helped prepare breakfast by scrambling the eggs into a creamy batter so Darcy could cook them. "A sour stomach again?"

"No, last night was bad. But today is better. The tea with mint helped."

"I'm glad to hear it. I imagine you'll want to be puttin' off teachin' the boys until this stage passes?"

"Then it will pass?" The news relieved her. She was weary of feeling this way.

"It did for me and Charleigh, when she carried Clemmie. I'm sure it will for you, too." Darcy regarded her with compassion, then quit her task to put a motherly arm around Sarah. "You're such a tiny thing, little more than a babe yourself."

Sarah might be young, but with all she'd endured, she felt as old as the wife of Tua, the chieftain of her mother's tribe. True, she had turned seventeen only months ago, but a few girls on her island had already nursed their first babies at Sarah's age.

Still, Darcy's gesture kindled a great need in Sarah, one missing ever since her mother died. The desperate urge to confide in someone overwhelmed her, and Darcy had been such a friend.

Quietly, Sarah spoke, admitting her weakness, telling her of all the lessons her aunt had taught and how horribly she'd failed. How she did not know how to be strong. How she knew Bill must resent her or pity her.

Darcy shook her head, her eyes wide in incredulity. "I 'ave never heard such a heap of horse rubbish in all me born days."

Wounded by the unexpected attack, Sarah began to withdraw.

Darcy's arm tightened. "No, no, not you, luv. As you know by now, I'm one t' speak me mind and often blurt things out without thinkin'. But I'm here to tell you, those teachings of your aunt's are pure rubbish. A man don't think less kindly of his wife just because he sees her cry. Well, most men don't, anyways, and I feel Bill is most men. If anything, it makes a man feel stronger, more of a protector—as a man needs to feel. And Bill surely doesn't look at you with pity or contempt! Not from what I've seen, he doesn't."

Recalling the stiffness on his face a moment ago, the ice frosting his blue eyes, Sarah shook her head. Darcy had not seen what she had seen.

"There now, never mind. I think your aunt misled you into believin' something that just isn't so. The strength that you need for the bad days you can't just pull up from inside you, Sarah. The strength has to come from somewhere on the outside. It doesn't just grow inside your belly, like the babe you carry. That strength is God, and it's Him you need to look to for help when times are hard."

Sarah vaguely nodded. "My father said that strength was Jehovah, and *Jehovah Rapha* means *the God who heals*."

"There now, you see!" Darcy pulled away, her eyes triumphant.

"But my aunt said that strength came from many gods. And she is a very strong woman. Cannot both my father and my aunt be right?"

Such a look of concerned pity filled Darcy's eyes that Sarah looked away, almost ashamed to air such a question. She felt so confused.

"I think Pastor Wilkins can better answer your questions and help you to understand more than I ever could, Sarah." Darcy gave a faint smile. "Say, why don't you come to Manhattan with Charleigh and meself? Stewart is taking us there next week. He needs to talk with a judge, and we women need to shop for trifles our small town doesn't carry. It might do you good to get away for a spell."

Sarah thought the matter over. "I'll talk with Bill."

"Good. Now I best be finishin' these eggs before I have fifteen hungry boys stampeding me kitchen! Be a love, and set the table, would you?"

Sarah nodded and set about the task, taking plates from the sideboard into the large dining room and laying them out on the two tables. She wished she could feel comforted, but it was hard for her to reconcile herself to the fact that Aunt Lefu could be mistaken when her aunt was so strong—harsh, many called it. For the past ten years, her aunt had taught her. Sarah wasn't sure if she could just throw all those teachings away.

thirteen

As he drove toward the pastor's home, Bill darted a glance to Sarah every now and then. Tendrils of black hair had come loose from her thick braid, stirred by the air from the open window. Her expression was serene; her face glowed as though she were imbued with life. He wondered if his mention of the picnic had brought that flush of color to her cheeks, that luminescence to her face. Earlier, she had caught him putting the hamper in the back of the Tin Lizzie, so he'd admitted his plan. For the first time, her eyes had sparkled with what looked like joy, and that gave Bill hope. Maybe he could win her heart sooner than he'd thought.

At the pastor's home a short and plump, gray-haired woman opened the door. She smiled effusively and greeted Sarah with open eagerness. "My husband told me all about meeting the two of you last Sunday. I'm so excited to know you, Sarah, and I look forward to long talks with you about your island." Her green eyes sparkled. "As I'm sure my husband told you, I thrive on adventure. My great-grandfather was a sea captain. My grandfather was a general in the War Between the States. My father was a hot-air balloon enthusiast. And I married a preacher." She laughed delightedly. "Believe me when I tell you, *that* is an adventure of and unto itself."

Pastor Wilkins cleared his throat from the opposite side of the room. "I see you've all met." He gave a tolerant but loving look to his wife. "My dear, would you bring us some tea?"

"Of course, dear." Her look was just as affectionate as she whisked away.

Something twisted inside Bill, making him hungry for such

camaraderie between himself and Sarah. On the island, they'd come midway to that point. He hoped that today would be the start of reaching it in full.

Several chairs stood close in the small parlor, where Pastor Wilkins had laid out his notes and a Bible. Once settled, he went over the notes of Sunday's meeting, also bringing up the first commandment: "Thou shalt have no other gods before me."

Bill listened, as interested as Sarah. He noticed that at times her brow clouded, as if she were confused or uncertain. Pastor Wilkins patiently answered her many questions and took her still further through the Bible, showing her in 1 Kings how those kings who did evil in the sight of the Lord and who worshiped idols were punished. But those who did good and worshiped only the Lord God were blessed. His wife brought tea and swept quietly out again. While they drank the hot beverage, Pastor Wilkins clarified and taught and listened. Bill was impressed with the man. He was as new to this as Sarah, but after an hour in the pastor's company, he didn't see how she could question any longer.

"If what you say is truly wrong. . ." Sarah's eyes clouded. "Why then do my people take part in such things? They are good men and women; they seek only to do what is right."

Bill felt a stab of apprehension. This was the first he'd ever heard her refer to them as her people and not as her mother's people. In an instant, he realized just how strong the connection was to her aunt and why this was so difficult for her.

"Didn't you tell me that your father is a missionary?" The pastor looked confused.

"Yes, but many of the villagers do as he tells them with their lips and actions only; they do not believe in the Christian God with their hearts—though there are some who do."

"And what do you believe, Sarah?"

"I believe in Jesus, the Christ, and in all He did. I believe He is God."

"Well, that's the first step." The pastor looked relieved. "But anyone can believe. You have to receive Him into your heart and life."

"I believe I have done this. I have accepted Jesus as my own. But for years, my aunt has taught me another way, and I have visited her temple."

"And your father allowed this?" There was no mistaking the pastor's shock.

Sarah briefly looked down at her lap, her brows sadly drawn together. "For a long time, my father turned away from God after my mother died. He allowed me to go where I wished and took little notice of me. His sorrow was very great. After he returned to God, at times he tried to tell me what you speak now. But I didn't understand and told him so, since in the time of his great sorrow he never denied me attending the ceremonies or learning from my aunt."

Sarah remembered the look of agony that had crossed her father's face at her quiet words of confusion. The tears that had filled his eyes. He had hugged her close, then swiftly turned and left the hut.

The pastor thought a long moment. "Sarah, do you have access to a Bible?"

"My father sent his Bible with me, and I read some on the ship. I have not finished it."

At this, the pastor's lips quirked at the corners. "Yes, it does take some time to reach that point. I have written down some scriptures and would like you to study them. I could read them to you, but I've found it helps when one looks at the passages for oneself. My methods might seem odd to some of my calling, but this is what I've determined works best."

Sarah took the paper. "I will do as you ask."

The pastor talked with them a while longer; then his wife popped in to bring cookies and more tea. Sarah barely nibbled at her shortbread wafer. Suddenly she looked up, her eyes hopeful.

"May I have a pickle?"

All of them stared at her—whether for her lack of social decorum or her odd request Bill didn't know. He supposed he shouldn't be too surprised. For a woman whose daily diet had often included octopus and eel, a sour pickle with tea wasn't so unusual. Feeling Sarah withdraw just by noting the way her body slightly recoiled and her chin lowered, as if embarrassed, Bill spoke up. "If it wouldn't be too much trouble, I'd like a pickle, too."

&

Once they left the pastor's home, Sarah let out a relieved sigh. The woman didn't have any pickles, unlike Darcy, who bought them from the grocer on a regular basis, and Sarah wished now she hadn't given in to this strange craving of the dills and asked for one. Although the pastor's wife didn't say a word and treated her just as kindly as when Sarah had walked through the front door, questioning her about the island, Sarah realized she'd committed a social error.

Bill was quieter, directing a sort of sad smile her way now and again. She buried a sigh, knowing she must have disappointed him.

At her first view of the lake, Sarah exhaled softly. It wasn't home, with its breadfruits and palms, its tropical flowers, and waterfall, but this place contained a beauty and peace all its own that soothed Sarah's soul. Trees of lush green surrounded a shimmering body of water. Sunlight pushed through leafy boughs and glanced off the water, gilding it in ripples. Quiet birdsong filled the trees.

Bill led the way to a grassy area and laid a blanket on the ground. Sarah ignored the blanket and moved to the edge of the lake. The call of the water, which she had so missed, enticed her, and she sat down to pull off the uncomfortable narrow pumps that all the women in New York wore.

"Sarah?"

Next came off her stockings.

"What are you doing?" His voice was dazed. "That water must be near freezing. I wouldn't try it if I were you. The lake could be deep."

She hesitated, torn between his words and the desire to feel moving water around her again. She gave him a hopeful smile. "Surely it is not as deep as an ocean?"

He stared at her several more seconds, then gave a slight permissive nod.

Sarah tested the waters. Bill was right; it chilled her senses but at the same time revived them. To feel the water lap over her bare foot freed something inside her. Seeing that the edge was shallow and allowed for her to wade in, she bunched up her dress around her hips and did so.

"Sarah. . ." His voice held a note of caution. "Be careful."

The clear water rushed gently past her legs as if welcoming her, and she almost wept with how good it felt. She waded out farther until the hem of her dress absorbed the water. What she would give to swim again, though in this long dress such a feat was unlikely.

She stood awhile longer, then, with a sigh, retraced her steps to Bill, who'd not altered from his position or from staring at her. She sensed pain in his eyes before he turned his attention to the picnic hamper.

"Let's see what Darcy packed for us, shall we?" His tone came light, though his shoulders looked heavy.

Sarah collected her stockings and shoes and joined him on the blanket, hoping she had not upset him. His stance seemed distant, though his words welcomed her.

"Sandwiches—ham, by the looks of it. Fruit—knowing Darcy, that's no surprise." He pulled out a container. "And here are your pickles!"

"Thank you." Sarah smiled as she took the container and the sandwich he offered.

Bill opened the wrapper and picked up his own sandwich, opening his mouth in readiness for a bite, then glanced at Sarah, who sat still, calmly waiting.

"What?" he asked.

"Should we not offer thanks?"

"Zowie! You're right. I'm still new at this." He set down his sandwich and bowed his head as Sarah did, offering a short prayer.

"Tell me," she asked as she ate her sandwich, glad her stomach didn't rebel and she could eat again. "Is *zowie* slang?"

"Sure is. Means full of zip." At her blank look, he added, "Energy."

"Will you teach me more of this slang, Bill? I should like to know it."

The conversation between them lightened considerably as Bill did just that, making Sarah laugh at the slang words and their meanings. He taught her slang phrases for any person who was remarkable, comically pantomiming "the bee's knees," "the elephant's eyebrows," "the snake's hips," and more, until she was laughing so hard tears rolled from her eyes.

When he got down on all fours and pantomimed "the cat's meow," and actually sidled near her, purring, she had the craziest urge to pet him and did lift her hand. Before she went through with it, however, she realized what she was doing and slowly withdrew it. He seemed not to notice and went on to show her "the gnat's elbow" and "the cat's pajamas."

Thoroughly entertained by her husband's silly antics, Sarah felt the first stirrings of hope that their marriage could flourish, based on friendship alone, if not love.

Though on her part, she would always love Bill.

fourteen

Three days later, Bill stood on the porch and thought a lot about that picnic. It was the first time he'd seen and heard Sarah laugh again, really laugh. Like she had during her ride on her pet dolphin. And he'd purposely striven for humor, acting like a sap, just to hear her delight. The ring of her laughter made him feel good inside.

The screen door creaked open, and he turned his head. Brent joined him on the porch, coming to stand beside him. Both men stared straight ahead.

"I came to inquire as to whether you're feeling well," Brent said. "You were quiet at dinner."

Bill chuckled. "I'm surprised you noticed. With fifteen boys chattering away, dinnertime can't exactly be described as silent in this place."

"Yes, that is one area on which we still have improvements to make. The newest additions to the refuge instigate questions and incite the others to trouble."

"Chad and Roland?"

Brent nodded. "They do more than instigate questions, I'm sorry to say. Being brothers, they often urge one another to dissension."

"They play off one another." Bill thought about that. "I've noticed Chad tends to be more of a leader. They seem very close. I rarely see them apart."

"They are close."

The words Brent spoke didn't seem to be all about Chad and Roland, and Bill felt his brother nurtured the same thoughts he did. In speaking of the two boys, Bill couldn't help but be reminded of how close he and Brent once were, Brent always playing follower to Bill's leader.

"We did have some good times, didn't we?" Bill let out a sigh of reminiscence.

Brent's expression became nostalgic. "We did."

The desire to rectify past mistakes spurred Bill to speak. "But we can never go back, can we?"

Brent hesitated. "It's not always wise to revisit the past, no."

Bill closed his eyes, the crushing blow of defeat bowing his shoulders. He had so wanted not only to make amends with his brother and ask for his forgiveness, but also he'd hoped to rekindle the strong friendship they'd once shared. Though his brother had accepted him back, had even been friendly, he maintained a wary distance.

Again, Bill wondered if he would always be chained to his past sins. God had forgiven him and accepted him, though he was in no way as good a Christian as his brother and Stewart were, and he doubted he would ever be considered worthy enough to have the town regard him with respect. Still, he had hoped that at some point Brent could move beyond the past and give Bill another chance to be his brother, as close as they'd once been.

Before Bill could retreat to the house, Brent spoke. "Perhaps it's not my place to ask this, but given the fact you did come to me for advice, I don't feel as if I'm treading on forbidden ground." He cleared his throat. "I trust matters have improved between you and your wife?"

Bill wished he could give him a positive response, but the truth was he just didn't know. "She seemed to enjoy the picnic and the lake."

"Yes, so I've heard. Darcy tells me she has visited the lake every day since you took her there."

Bill eyed him in shock. "She has? How did she get there? She doesn't know how to drive a car or wagon."

"Apparently, she walked. As the lake is off the road, it's not difficult to find."

Bill shouldn't have been surprised Sarah went on foot those two miles, since she'd engaged in more walking than that every day when on her island. But the impulsive, unpredictable actions of his young wife never failed to astonish him. Part woman, part child, Sarah excited and delighted him. *I'd do anything if I could have her love. I just don't know what to do anymore to get it.*

"Perhaps you're trying too hard?"

Bill hadn't realized he'd spoken, and he looked at Brent in surprise.

"Love is a gentle fragrance, Bill. As delicate as the sweet scent of a rose. It cannot be forced, nor can it be captured. It blossoms when it's ready, and when that day arrives, the fragrance stirs the senses in ways that cannot be expressed or imagined."

Brent's words moved him. "You always were such a poet." His remark was not unkind. "Yet what if that rose never blossoms. Then what?"

Brent actually grinned. His eyes seemed to sparkle behind his spectacles. "Somehow, Bill, I don't think you have cause for concern in that regard."

Bill realized his brother had no idea of the truth, since he didn't know all the facts, including that his and Sarah's marital relations were nonexistent. And he felt it was time to change the subject. "Can I ask a question?"

Brent inclined his head in an inviting manner.

"What's the story behind the spectacles? Sometimes you have them on, sometimes you carry them in your pocket."

"The twins have a tendency to grab for them."

Brent's face flushed, and Bill grinned, suddenly realizing the true reason Brent went without them far more than he wore them. He'd overheard Darcy comment to Brent how much she liked his eyes, and Bill felt the absence of the spectacles must have something to do with that.

Bill looked out over the yard. A few of the boys who'd been working there now stared toward the thicket that led to the road. Their mouths hung open as they gawked, standing as though turned into living statues.

Bill looked that way. His heart jumped, then dropped.

Sarah came walking toward them, barefoot, her long hair damp, loose, and hanging to her thighs. Instead of the gray dress she usually wore, she had reverted to her islandwear and wore her red, knee-length sarong.

"Hello." Her smile was uncertain as she reached them.

Brent turned. His eyes went wide in shock before he hurriedly looked away. "I should go grade some essays. Good day, Sarah. Bill." Quickly he escaped into the house.

Sarah halted. "I have done something wrong?" The worry on her face did not escape Bill's notice.

He should explain to his wife about conventions concerning dress and what was considered appropriate. Her father had let her run too wild on that island. Noticing that the boys continued to gawk, he called out to them. "Don't you have chores that need tending to?"

A few looked away and resumed their work. But the rest continued to stare.

He took hold of Sarah's arm, pulling her with him into the house. "You should change clothes. You must be cold."

"I'm not cold."

"Well, you should change clothes anyway."

"I have done something to displease you?"

Her soft anxious words gave Bill pause, and he forced himself to calm. "Don't you like the dress I bought you?" He continued walking with her up the stairs.

"I cannot swim in it."

"Swim?" He looked at her, though he shouldn't be surprised. They reached their bedroom, and he brought her with him inside, away from the prying ears of anyone curious enough to listen.

"You do not approve?"

He felt her withdrawal, saw the hurt disappointment in her eyes. When had her eyes ever been so revealing? Her face was awash with emotion, showing her feelings as she never had before except on the day she left her father. And he realized this must be very important to her. How could he deny her this one request when she'd given up so much by leaving her island and those she loved?

"I suppose it's all right for you to visit the lake and swim. I know how much you love the water." He sighed, leaned against the door. "But from now on, I want you to take the other dress with you and change into it before you return to the refuge."

She looked down at her sarong, then up at him again. "Does the dress displease you, Bill?"

The dress definitely did not displease him. Forcing himself to look away from her slender curves and shapely calves, he stared into her eyes. They held such a look of distressed confusion, and he knew he wasn't going about this at all well. Maybe Darcy or Charleigh could explain about social propriety if he asked. He was sure they wouldn't mind.

"Please, just change into the dress I bought you, Sarah."

He managed a stiff smile before leaving the room. As he strode downstairs, a sense of irony struck him. He had never conformed to strict conventions or society's stiff rules. Yet those ideas altered the moment he saw those boys gawking at his wife. Even though he knew she'd been blameless in her actions, he hadn't liked the attention she received. Not one bit. Odd that he, who'd once snubbed his nose at the law and everything about it, was now all in favor of protocol. Bill shook his head in stupefied amusement at the changed man he'd become.

Life, indeed, was an irony.

❧

With no one to see her, Sarah let the tears run down her cheeks as she changed into the ugly gray dress. Never had she imagined her simple sarong would cause such a stir. Bill never said anything about it on the island. But then, New York was so different from her island.

She sighed and picked up the cross, again looking at its symbols. Under the one showing her mother's death had been carved another one—the sun, weak and far to the corner. The crown at the opposite corner showed the distance that had come between her and her father, no doubt. But between them was what looked like a snake.

She frowned. A snake?

Snakes symbolized evil, according to her father. She wondered why he would show evil had come between them.

A knock at the door broke her from her musings. "Yes?"

Charleigh entered, smiling. "I hope you don't mind if I visit for a bit. Bill thought you might like to talk."

"Of course." Sarah laid down the cross and watched as Charleigh came to sit beside her on the bed. Her bright red hair shone as the sun hit it, reminding Sarah of one of the beautiful tropical flowers on her island. The woman was so beautiful in both features and spirit. Since the day Sarah had come here, Charleigh had shown her nothing but kindness.

"I heard about what happened." Charleigh's green eyes conveyed sympathy. "I know things are difficult for you, adapting to a new way of life, but I want you to know I'm here to help you as you learn. And I'd like to explain how things are here in America, so it will help you understand what just happened and why everyone acted so strangely."

She went on to explain about conventions and that hemlines to the knees were looked upon with horror—protocol stated they must remain below the calves, though some people didn't even approve of that and were horrified by the rising hemlines. As she spoke, her gaze went to both the drab dress Sarah wore and the colorful one she'd laid across a chair. "It's very pretty."

"Thank you. I made it myself. On the island, many of the women wear clothes of such color, of many different hues." Sarah sighed.

Charleigh fingered the cloth. She looked back at the gray-checked dress, then to the sarong, her gaze thoughtful. "As the months progress, you'll need new clothing at any rate. Darcy told me about your condition, and I'm so happy for you. She also mentioned that she invited you to join us when we go to Manhattan next week." She brightened. "We could visit the boutique and buy you a lovely dress, Sarah. You would look pretty in green or blue."

Sarah lowered her head. "I am not certain Bill would approve."

"I think he would adore you in those colors."

"No, I mean about going to Manhattan. When I have spoken of the city in the past, he became very quiet. I think he has bad memories there."

"Would you like Stewart to talk with him?"

Sarah considered the offer. "If he wouldn't mind, yes. I should like to go with you to the city." Charleigh and Darcy had become such good friends. To be in their close company for a day might take some of the burden of loneliness off Sarah's heart caused by her husband's distance.

≈

"No." Bill's reply came swift and forceful.

Stewart's eyes flashed in surprise. But then, Bill reasoned, the man couldn't know the dangers of what he asked. The two sat on chairs on the porch. Bill often came here to relax, yet the suddenness of Stewart's question caused him to tense.

Stewart was silent a moment. "Perhaps you might think it over? The women really enjoy a day of shopping in Manhattan.

I try to bring them with me whenever business takes me there, and I must meet with a judge about an important matter concerning one of the boys he put in my care."

Bill admired this man who had done so much for so many child delinquents. "You take from all the courts then?"

"My former position as a lawyer puts me in contact with many from that establishment." He looked straight at Bill. "I take those no one wants, those the court has given up on, and I try to give them a home, hope, and a second chance."

"Your place reminds me of another charity I've heard about. Boys Town. Ever hear of it?"

"In Omaha." Stewart nodded. "A worthy institution. My desire is to one day provide even more room to house the children who need help. There are so many wandering souls out there." He looked out over the trees, his expression distant.

"You do a good job with what you have."

Another stretch of silence came between them.

"If you're worried that the women will be unaccompanied, I assure you, you have no cause for concern." Stewart glanced at Bill. "Except for the short time I leave them under the care of the boutique's manager, I'm with them at all times."

Bill carefully considered his next words. He'd been at the refuge almost two months, had hoped to put more time behind him before touching on those days, but maybe the moment had come for him to share a snippet of his dark past that refused to remain buried in his mind. With Stewart, who'd become an acquaintance but still considered Bill a stranger, he could. With Brent, who'd once been a close brother but still considered Bill a traitor, he could not. He still felt the distance between him and his brother.

"When I left Manhattan more than a year ago, I left in a hurry." He collected his thoughts, realizing Stewart already knew this. "I worked for a family involved in the underworld. Never mind what I did; I'm sure you can fill in the blanks, and you'd be right no matter what you put in them."

Stewart gave a short, comprehending nod.

"There was trouble within the family. One of the sons was doing a double cross—er, betraying his father. He wanted all the power—something you often find in that kind of racket. Thirst for power." Bill stared out across the lawn, finding it easier to look at the trees ahead than at Stewart. "I was what you would call stuck in the middle. I'd saved the man's son once, and well, even though an outsider never becomes part of the family, that doesn't mean they still don't work for them."

"I do understand, Bill. I was a Manhattan lawyer, remember."

"Right." Bill blew out a breath. "Okay, well, it's like this. I drove Vittorio's son to a meeting place. He was involved in some underhanded dealings with the enemy—another crime family—and, things went bad. Real bad. Vittorio's son got shot, and someone on the outside saw me with a gun. The real killers vamoosed before they were seen, and I was left holding the bag. Word leaked back to Vittorio that I'd been the one to shoot his son. Thing is, he never would have believed Marco was anything but loyal. Marco was a convincing liar. But one doesn't go up to the crime boss and say, "Sorry, you got the wrong fellow"—one runs. Because if you don't, you're a dead man. When you hurt one of the family, you have just nailed your own coffin shut."

Stewart remained silent a moment. "I understand your reason for leaving the country. But I don't understand why you're concerned about Sarah visiting Manhattan with us. You told Brent that Vittorio's family thinks you're dead."

Stewart's reasoning was sound, yet Bill couldn't help feel a niggling fear.

"No one from Vittorio's family knows Sarah is your wife. I shall take the women into Manhattan and be with them almost continually, and I do know how to protect if confronted,

Bill. However, I sincerely doubt that even if a member of Vittorio's crime family were to see Sarah, they would make the connection that she was your wife. They don't know us, either. We'll just be another group of people among the thousands there."

"May I ask why you're so strongly in favor of taking Sarah?"

Grinning, Stewart gave a helpless shrug. "It's important to Charleigh, and what's important to her is important to me. I want to do whatever is in my power to see her happy. She and Darcy enjoy shopping in the boutiques, and since I take them no more than twice a year, it's a special event."

A sense of sadness swept into Bill's heart. Stewart and Charleigh. Brent and Darcy. Obviously two couples so much in love. He wanted the same with Sarah. He could feel that vacancy in his life that much more strongly when he stood in the others' presence and witnessed their adoring glances, the small touches they gave to one another. A loving hand on the back, a gentle touch on the arm.

Bill sighed. "Do you think I don't care about Sarah's happiness?"

"Not at all. I know you do. But at the same time, I think you're being overprotective, which is natural, considering what you went through. But that was over a year ago, Bill, and they assume you're dead. This is one day in Manhattan."

Stewart's tall muscular frame and no-nonsense attitude helped to relieve any doubts about his ability to protect the women. But a man's build or size didn't factor in when talking about guns. A bullet could down the strongest man alive.

Yet Bill knew Vittorio's family wouldn't gun them down in the street. That wasn't how the family operated. Their ways were more underhanded and sneaky, less public.

"Give me a few days to think it over," Bill amended. "I just can't give you an answer right now."

"Fair enough." Stewart rose to his feet. "I had better get back to the book work."

Bill said nothing, his mind active as it visited the past once again.

fifteen

Sarah was excited to visit the church again, her embarrassment over her social error no longer disturbing. After Darcy had shared some mistakes she'd made when she'd first arrived at the refuge, Sarah laughed and felt much better about her own awkward moments.

As she and Bill approached the church, a sudden faint yipping sound came from behind her. She turned at the same moment a brown puppy scampered up to her on awkward legs. It jumped against her ankles. The little animal was so tiny, so cute, she had no fear of it and bent to gather the warm furry bundle into her hands.

"Why, hello!" She brought it closer to her. Its pink tongue began bathing her face. There had been dogs of a type on her island but none as cute as this little fellow.

"Uh, Sarah. . ." At Bill's low words, she looked up. He stared at someone beyond her, then turned his attention to her. "Maybe we should go inside?"

Sarah glanced in the direction Bill had been looking. An elderly woman Sarah remembered as Mrs. Cosgrove stared at Sarah in shocked disdain, then lifted her head high and entered the church.

Heart deflated, Sarah looked back at Bill. "Playing with dogs before a church meeting is not allowed in society's rules?"

A tender expression crossed his face. "No, you go ahead and enjoy that pup. I think his owner is coming this way."

Sarah held onto the wriggling bundle, smiling down into his affectionate brown eyes, but a morsel of the joy had been lost. Bill was being kind; she had obviously embarrassed him again. The pup licked her face, bringing back her smile. She watched as Bill walked over to a young boy and talked with him. The child made a lot of motions with his hands, pointing behind him, pointing toward her and the pup. Bill soon returned with the boy in tow.

"Sorry about that, ma'am." The boy held his hands out for the pup. "Little guy gets loose a lot when my brother leaves the barn door open. He was the runt of the litter, though as fast as he runs now, you'd never believe it."

Sarah smiled acknowledgment to the child as Bill led her into church, and they slipped into a pew. The service was as stimulating as the last one she'd attended. The hymns of worship blessed her soul, especially the song "All Hail the Power of Jesus' Name," and she longed to learn the music so she could sing along as well. The pastor's message from 1 Corinthians dealt with unconditional love and spoke to her heart. She was again reminded of her father both in the way the pastor delivered the sermon and by his friendly attitude.

Afterward, the pastor's wife and the organist sought Sarah out to speak with her while Bill excused himself. Curious about what was so important that it couldn't wait until they reached the refuge, Sarah watched as he talked to his brother and Stewart. Perhaps Bill felt uncomfortable being the sole male in a group of women now clustered around her. Though these women were kind, Sarah couldn't help but notice the snubs she received from other parishioners, women and men alike. She kept the mask of cool detachment on her features, but the slights wounded, and she wondered if they had listened to today's message.

Darcy came up to the group, nodded a greeting to the others, then looked at Sarah. "Bill asked that we take you home with us. One of the boys is sick and we need to return. Sorry, luv."

"Bill's not coming?"

"He said he'll meet us at the refuge."

"Oh." Sarah wasn't sure what to think or why Bill would simply vanish like that, but she accompanied Darcy to the waiting car and was silent the entire ride home.

Once at the refuge, she went to her room, restless, and picked up the cross. She looked at the symbol below the last one—the crown seemed to hang in limbo and at a titled angle, the sun much smaller and far away, the snake larger— then she again set it on the table. She didn't want to think what it meant, though she suspected she knew. Her aunt had brought darkness into her life, according to what her father and those at Lyons' Refuge thought. And after reading all of 1 Kings and other passages in the Bible that Pastor Wilkins had recommended, Sarah was beginning to feel as if her father was right.

She loved her aunt; that would never change. But as she'd read the words of life, the conviction deep within her spirit could not be ignored. She recognized truth in them and now felt cheated. Sarah had needed guidance. Her father had been unable to give it. Her aunt had provided it, and now Sarah realized all that she'd been taught was wrong. Much of it was considered wicked, and she felt as if a rift had been ripped open inside her. A part of her childhood and young girlhood must be torn away from her in order for her to please the Lord. Though she desired to serve Christ, she couldn't help but feel bitter tears well up for all she'd learned and lost.

It did no good to question why these events happened. She didn't blame her father for his lack of fatherly wisdom or withdrawal during those two years; she knew his love for her mother had been immense. As a child, she'd felt such reassurance, such happiness to see them together. Her mother had been a soft-spoken woman, but she, too, spoke of faith in the Lord to Sarah. At the memory, Sarah wondered what had drawn her to listen to her aunt, when her own mother had been a Christian convert.

The rattling sound of an automobile coming up the path drew her to the window. She frowned when she saw the Tin Lizzie swerve from side to side a couple of times, as though Bill worked to keep it on the dirt path.

She hurried downstairs, wondering if he was ill. As she walked out the door, Bill exited the vehicle, his smile so wide it captured her heart and her breath, and then her gaze lowered to the wriggling brown ball of fur in his hands.

"He's for you, Sarah." Bill held out the puppy to her. "Your new pet."

She gasped. Stunned at his thoughtfulness, she felt tears glaze her eyes. Her heart felt so full she thought she might float away. Without thought, without hesitation, she went to him, rose up on her toes, and, laying one hand on his shoulder, gently kissed his cheek.

ô

Bill stood on the porch hours later, touching the cheek that Sarah had kissed. He still could hardly believe she'd done that. Afterward she'd seemed embarrassed and had drawn back, though her smile was genuine as she took the squirming pup who'd been christened with the name Sasi. All through the drive from the previous owner's, Bill had worked to hold onto the writhing ball of fur, almost driving off the road a few times as the Tin Lizzie chugged along. The animal had even wet on his trousers in its excitement, but the ordeal had been worth it to see the look in Sarah's eyes. And to receive the gift of her kiss.

He inhaled deeply, then headed inside. Charleigh sat in a rocker with Clementine, humming a song to her.

"Any idea where Sarah is?"

"I think she went to the lake."

"This late?" Bill didn't like the sound of that. Only a few hours remained until sunset. "Mind if I borrow the car?"

"Oh, I'm sorry, Bill. Stewart took it into town. And Samuel and Greg are working on the other one. The brake sticks."

"Okay. Thanks." He headed out the door, wondering what to do. Well, his wife made the walk every day. He didn't suppose it would hurt him, and hopefully he would run into her coming back.

The summer day was mild, but by the time he got to the lake, the water looked inviting. More so, with his wife in it. Unnoticed, Bill stood beneath the trees and watched.

She laughed and played with the puppy as it waded near her, slowly dog-paddling in circles before it moved to shore. The pup padded out and shook itself briskly before scampering to the gray dress to sniff it. Seeing Bill, it ran at an angle toward him and jumped about his ankles a few times. Absently he reached down to pet it, while keeping his eye out for his wife, who had immediately dived under the water once her pet left her. The pup went to make a bed in the gray dress.

Sarah broke the surface, and Bill watched her swim in her sarong, her movements graceful, alluring. Once he'd resisted the pull to join her in the water, at the island, but now he accepted the push that sent him wanting to rush to her. Heart beating fast, he bent to pull off his shoes.

❧

Reveling in the feel of the silky water around her skin, Sarah swam with delight. After a while, the water was no longer cold, and she loved to spend her afternoons here. She glided underneath and resurfaced to swim on her back. The top of her head hit something solid. More than curious, she swirled around and came face to face with Bill!

She blinked, a short pause ensued, and then he grinned.

"Ever had a water fight?" His tone came out boyish, innocent, as he sprayed her with water.

Laughing, she threw her hands up to cover her eyes. "Bill!"

He didn't relent in his playful attack, and she squealed,

ducked, then came up with a spray of her own and splashed him with it. Thoroughly enjoying herself, she laid back and kicked the water so it showered in his face.

"All right, you. . ." His look of mock retribution as he steadily advanced had her squealing again, and she tried to swim away. He slid underneath the water and grabbed her legs, pulling her down and dunking her beneath with him.

They came up for air, Sarah laughing. They were close, closer than before. Her heart thudded with expectation at the look that suddenly entered his eyes, and the mood between them changed, going from playful to electric.

"Sarah," he whispered before his lips touched hers.

She felt as if she were floating and falling at the same time and wrapped her arms around his neck, both to anchor herself and keep from sinking. His arms drew her closer. Their kisses took her heart to a place she'd known only one other night. . . .

" 'Won't you come home, Bill Bailey, won't you come home— she cried the whole night lo-ong.' "

The sudden sound of two boys singing at the top of their lungs, and badly, startled them and broke them apart. They turned to the bushes to see Joel and Herbert, their hands pressed to their hearts in mock-dramatic flair as they belted out the tune. The pup woke up from its nap and began barking.

" 'I'll do the cookin' darlin',' " Joel sang in high falsetto, turning to Herbert.

" 'I'll pay the rent,' " Herbert answered back in a deeper voice than normal.

" 'I knows I done you wrong,' " they both crooned, clasping both hands and holding them to their hearts as they each put their weight on one leg and leaned toward the other, heads held high, while facing Sarah and Bill.

Bill closed his eyes and groaned. Sarah couldn't help but giggle.

" 'Remember, that rainy evening I threw you out, with

nothin' but a fine-toothed comb,' " Joel sang. Then together they gave their finale, " 'I know I'se to blame, well, ain't that a shame—Bill Bailey won't you please, Bill Bailey won't you please, Bill Bailey won't you pleeease come hooome!' " Joel swept off his cap from his fair hair, and both boys bowed deeply from the waist.

Bill shook his head. "Don't you kids have anything better to do than to spy on your elders?" Tenseness edged the humor of his words, and Sarah looked at him.

"Aw, we weren't doing no spying," Herbert said. "Honest. Ain't that right, Joel?"

"That's right. Mr. Lyons asked where you were, and since we were out berry-picking anyways for Miss Darcy so she can make her pies, we told him we'd look for you." He picked up a pail that was at his feet. "See?" Herbert picked up his, too.

"Well, you found me. Your message is delivered, so you can both skedaddle now."

"Didn't know we'd find you in the middle of the lake though." Joel's angelic face couldn't hide his mischief. Herbert sniggered.

"Yeah, yeah." Bill let go of Sarah and made as if he was coming their way. "Don't make me have to tell you twice."

Joel's grin was wide. "Come on, Herbert. We know when we're not wanted." The boys took off, laughing and singing another round of the same song.

Bill shook his head. "Young scamps."

Sarah's heart settled back in her chest, lower than before. "You don't like children, Bill?"

"Never been around that many to know." He looked back at her, a look of resigned disappointment on his face. "Come on. We should be getting back anyway. The sun will soon set, and I don't like the idea of you walking home alone in the dark. I'd rather from now on you didn't come out here this late." He waded out of the water to the shore.

She watched him a few seconds, then followed. The beautiful moment between them had been shattered, but not just because of the boys' sudden entrance. She would do anything to recapture what she and Bill had just shared. He turned his back to her as she changed into the dry dress, then he took the wet one from her and they set out for the refuge. Yet even though they walked side by side, Bill seemed distant once again.

&

"Bill, I'd like you to meet Charleigh's father. This is Michael Larkin. He's a strong supporter of the refuge."

" 'Tis a pleasure to meet with ye, Bill."

Bill shook the man's hand, admiring his strong grasp. An Irishman by the sound of his voice, his obvious strength belied his years. And his tact was commendable, as well.

When Bill and Sarah returned from the lake, Bill in wet clothes and Sarah with her hair wet around her hips, the husky, gray-haired man who'd been sitting on the porch hadn't batted an eyelid. Of course, considering the craziness that went on at the refuge on a continual basis, maybe a grown man in dripping trousers and shirt wasn't all that odd to see.

"He's coming to Manhattan with us in a few days," Stewart went on to explain. "We've decided to stay overnight. Michael wants to treat us to a Broadway show. I think Sarah would enjoy that, as well as seeing some of the sights. And while I'm talking to Judge Markston, Michael will be staying with the ladies so they'll never be alone."

Bill directed a sharp glance at Stewart, to which the man shook his head. "No, I didn't tell him your story. But I don't think he'll be too shocked. Charleigh served a term in prison, remember, and at one time she also had a killer after her. Your brother saved both Darcy and Charleigh from his vengeful agenda."

"My brother?" Bill's eyes grew wide.

"Yes. In a most ingenious way, too. Got a black eye and split lip for his efforts. As a matter of fact, I think the killer was a former associate of yours—Philip Rawlins, though we knew him as Eric."

Bill stood rooted to the spot. "Phil came here?"

"It's a long story. One day I'll have to tell you about it."

A wash of emotions swept over Bill. Disbelief that his brother could find the courage needed to face a killer and save the women. Shock that the killer was the man Bill had once saved. Vittorio had marked Philip as a dead man, and Bill had warned him in advance. He shook his head, trying to get a grip on reality. It all seemed so bizarre.

"I also had a run-in with Eric years ago, and saved Charleigh from his clutches before you knew him. He's in jail last I heard. And while Brent won't be coming with us since he has to teach the boys, I want to assure you again that Sarah will be safe. We won't let her out of our sight."

Bill felt his defenses weakening. Stewart knew how to make a convincing argument. If Brent could and did protect the women, Bill certainly knew these men could.

"I'll think more on it." It was the best he could do.

sixteen

With her hair again braided into a more acceptable style, Sarah left the bedroom. She stopped upon hearing Charleigh's beautiful voice wafting down the corridor in a soothing tune.

" 'Too-ra-loo-ra-loo-ral. . .too-ra-loo-ra-li. . . Too-ra-loo-ra-loo-ral. . . Hush now, don't you cry. . . .' "

Sarah came to the threshold of Charleigh and Stewart's bedroom and peeked in, not wanting to disrupt the poignant moment. Charleigh sat in a rocker, smiling down at Clementine, who lay in her arms. The child's wide eyes looked up at her. Her hair, a shade lighter than her mother's, shone copper red.

" 'Too-ra-loo-ra-loo-ral. . .too-ra-loo-ra-li. . . Too-ra-loo-ra-loo-ral. . . That's an Irish lullaby. . . .' "

Tears came to Sarah's eyes as the haunting melody reached down deep to touch her soul, and she placed her hand to her stomach, hopeful for the day she would sing her own little one to sleep.

Charleigh looked up. Sarah, now embarrassed, turned away.

"Please don't go. Clemmie isn't being cooperative anyway. No lullaby created is going to put this one to sleep for her nap." Charleigh laid a fingertip to the child's nose, and she giggled.

Clementine twisted in her mother's lap and looked toward the doorway. She smiled, and Sarah's heart was touched. "May I hold her?"

Charleigh seemed surprised, but it was no wonder. Sarah had never offered to hold a child during all her weeks at the refuge. "Certainly. Maybe she just needs a change of hands to help her settle down." Charleigh rose from the rocker and handed the girl to her.

"Sa-rah," Clementine said with a smile, putting her little fingers on Sarah's cheek.

At that moment, something inside Sarah changed. Gone was the fear of impending motherhood and the fear of Bill's rejection of their child, while the entrance of motherly love captured her heart and soul. She desperately wanted her own baby to hold in her arms and almost wept with the release of the bonds that had constricted her from admitting that.

Searching for something to say to quell the rise of tears, she took the seat Charleigh had vacated and looked up at her. "This place, Lyons' Refuge, is such a place of song. Always I hear humming or singing from you or Darcy or even Stewart. And the boys shared a song with me and Bill today, as well."

She told her of it, and Charleigh laughed. "Not much of a surprise. That tune was a favorite years ago. We often play the phonograph of a Sunday or after the boys are bedded for the night."

"I come from an island of song," Sarah said wistfully as she began slowly rocking. "We are taught to dance with the song, to show its meaning. The boys' song reminded me of that, though at the same time it was nothing like it."

A sympathetic look crossed Charleigh's face. "Do you miss home very much, Sarah?"

"I do miss it; I miss my father most. But since I've come here, I feel a bond also to you at the refuge. The continual song, the Bible readings you hold every night, the openness and acceptance you have toward one another as family, all are so much of how my life was like on the island."

"I hope you know that we consider you family, too, Sarah. You're a part of us."

The words, soft and sincere, caressed Sarah. They gave her comfort that helped to heal the breach caused by her husband's frequent distance.

"How do I cause my husband to care for me?" Sarah stopped rocking, shocked that her deepest concern had come tumbling from her mouth.

Charleigh regarded her with some surprise. "I wouldn't think that was a problem where you and Bill are concerned."

Sarah shrugged one shoulder and started rocking again. "He is often distant. I fear it is because of my wea—because of something I may have done." She had almost spoken of her weakness. Remembering Darcy's reaction, she didn't want to invite further censure regarding her aunt. Sarah now understood that much of what Aunt Lefu taught had been wrong, but she did not wish to speak of it. The subject still distressed her.

Charleigh's smile was sad. "You two have been through a great deal these past months. Bill's escape from death, your marriage, and then leaving your home and father to come to a new land that holds bad memories for Bill. Hmm. . .I think what you two need is a little good old-fashioned romance. Take some time alone together, which is difficult to find at this place—how well I know! Perhaps tonight is a good time to bring out the phonograph. The moon seen from the porch is very conducive to romance. Stewart and I take advantage of it whenever we can find the opportunity." Charleigh grinned. "And tonight's moon should be full, which is even more romantic."

The thought of being in Bill's arms again sent Sarah's heart beating a little faster. She made an effort to slow her rocking, so as not to disturb Clementine, whose small head now rested against her shoulder, her eyes closed.

❧

Once the table had been cleared, the dishes washed, and the boys and other children had been sent to or tucked into their beds, Charleigh pulled a record from its sleeve and glanced toward Sarah and Bill. "I hear there's a gorgeous full moon outside this evening. Huge and bright."

Bill hadn't missed the loving smile Darcy and his brother had shared earlier, nor their quiet exit from the room. And now he didn't miss the way Stewart came up behind Charleigh and lowered his head to whisper something in her ear. She giggled like a schoolgirl, but her gaze remained fixed on Sarah and Bill.

"Air is nice and warm, too. A perfect night to take in the stars."

Bill looked at Sarah, his pulse going a bit unsteady both at the idea of having her to himself and the fear that she might refuse. "Would you like to step outside and take a look?"

"Yes, Bill."

His heart lurched at the shy, soft glow in her dark eyes, the hint of a smile on her upturned face. He swallowed, hardly daring to believe what he was seeing, feeling almost like a schoolboy again and not like a man courting his wife. "Okay." He grinned.

"That moon isn't getting any brighter," Stewart teased, and Charleigh playfully slapped his arm, which had snaked around her waist, though she was smiling.

Bill needed no further encouragement. He slipped his hand inside Sarah's and walked with her outside to the porch, then closed the door behind them.

He turned to look at her, but suddenly didn't know what to say. From inside, the scratchy sound of a record being played on the phonograph caught his attention. He watched Sarah as she glanced toward the sheer curtains. He cast a glance that way too. Stewart and Charleigh were dancing cheek to cheek.

Sarah turned her wide eyes upon him. He swallowed hard. "Would you care to dance, Sarah?"

"Yes, Bill." She held her hands out toward him, and he clasped one in his, slipping his other arm around her tiny waist. Slowly he danced with his wife, the porch too small for anything other than making tight circles. All the while they looked into one another's eyes.

"By the light of the silvery moon, I want to spoon, to my honey I'll croon love's tune. . . ." The music played on.

"Bill?"

"Yes, Sarah." His voice came soft.

"What is *spoon*? Is it slang, too?"

Her innocent question caused his heart to race, contrary to the slow movements they made as they danced. "Allow me to show you."

Bending down, he pressed his lips to hers in a kiss that revealed his heart. Sweet and passionate, tender and warm, the kiss continued until the end of the song. When Bill lifted his head, Sarah's eyes shone brightly.

"I like this word *spoon*."

He chuckled. "So do I."

When the record restarted, the two danced on. Bill pressed his cheek against her temple and her sleek hair, closing his eyes, inhaling the sweet fragrance of her.

"Sarah?"

"Yes, Bill?"

"I love you."

The words slipped out, begging for release. When only silence answered, Bill pushed down his disappointment, squeezing his eyes shut.

"I love you, too."

The words were as gentle as a whisper, but they triumphantly sounded a herald inside his mind. Clasping her upper arms, he pulled away to look at her.

"You love me?"

Her look was slightly puzzled. "Of course. I have loved you since we were on the island. Since I chose you for my husband."

Since I chose you. Bill blinked, astounded by the revelation.

He had not taken Sarah from her island. . .she had chosen to come with him. She had chosen *him*.

"You never said it before, never told me." Emotion made his voice rough. "That night on the ship, I told you I loved you then, but you didn't answer."

Her lips parted in amazement. "I never heard you." Her lashes swept down as though to conceal embarrassment, before looking up at him again. "But I was taught I should not express my feelings, that it was considered weak for a woman to do so. My aunt Lefu told me this."

"Well, your aunt was wrong." Bill could hardly believe what he was hearing. She loved him! All this time she had loved him. "Never think that you can't express your feelings to me, Sarah. Never. I want to know what you think and feel every moment. When you hurt, I want to know so I can share your pain; when you're happy, I want to know so I can share your joy. When you shut me out, it makes me feel as if I'm not important to you."

Her eyes widened at this, and he could tell such a thing had never occurred to her.

The irony of the moment—that all this time they'd each loved the other and neither had known it—struck him in the midst of the awe, and he gave a chuckle of disbelief. "It seems we've both been foolish. Maybe I was the real sap for not saying anything. You only did what you were taught; I should have known better. I've also loved you, maybe as far back as the day you made that deal with me to listen to the Bible, then told me about your island."

Such joy shone in her eyes, it took Bill's breath away. "Sarah. . ." Unable to hold back any longer, he kissed her again with tender passion.

"Your silvery beams will bring love dreams, we'll be cuddling soon, by the silvery moon. . ."

And as the song played on, they did just that.

❧

Sarah hummed as she went about her task. Morning sunlight streamed through the windows. As she made the bed, she looked at the two pillows close together and smiled. Since the night of the silvery moon, three evenings ago, life had changed. If she had ever doubted Bill's love for her, Sarah could do so no longer. Every action, every word, he gave from his heart, and Sarah blossomed. Even when he just looked at her from across the room, Sarah felt wrapped up in his embrace. And Sarah abandoned her aunt Lefu's teachings, instead showing her love for Bill. Yet for all their newfound delight in one another, a tremor of fear still plagued Sarah.

She still had not told him about the baby. Their shared love was too new, too fragile. If she told him and he retreated from her again, unhappy or upset about the news, she would wither like a rose without the nurturing water to keep it alive. She knew she must tell him soon, but each day that passed, she put it off. Her mind went to last night, as they had sat on the porch alone and looked at the stars. They'd sat on a porch glider, and he had held her within the circle of his arms.

"Sarah?" he'd asked. "Do you really want to go to Manhattan?"

Her heart jumped at the thought. "I would like to see more of it, to see a Broadway show, and to shop with Charleigh and Darcy, yes. I enjoy their company." She hesitated. "But I wish also that you would come."

He released a heavy sigh. "You know why I can't."

"I know." Sarah nestled her head against his shoulder. Last night, he had told her all about Vittorio and his former association with the mobster.

He let out another long, weighty breath. "If I allow you to go with them tomorrow, promise me you'll be very careful? That you'll stay close to Stewart or Michael at all times?"

She had looked up at him with surprise and reassurance.

"I will do what you ask."

As Sarah stood by the bed and remembered, she felt Bill's presence behind her. His arm slid around her waist, gently drawing her back to him. She sighed in love's sweet contentment. She didn't want to be separated from her husband, even though she would soon be with him again. Yet as the baby grew within her, she would need new clothes. For that reason alone, she must go, if for no other.

"What are you thinking about, pretty Sarah, to look so sad?"

She moved her hand to cover his. "That I do not look forward to being apart from you. Even for one night."

"Believe me. I don't relish the thought, either. But I've heard reunions can be wonderful." He nibbled at her ear.

She giggled, pleasure trickling through her at his touch.

He held her more tightly for a long moment, then let out a sigh and broke away. "I imagine they're waiting for you. I know Stewart wanted to get an early start to the station. Is your valise packed?"

She looked at the borrowed reticule that contained only a few items. "Yes."

"Sarah." When she didn't answer, he put his fingers to her chin and directed her gaze to his face. "I want you to have a good time. I want you to enjoy yourself. This is something your father wanted, for you to see how this culture lives, to take in the sights. He told me so."

Smiling, she nodded, yet she couldn't help but feel the distance even though they weren't parted yet. A premonition of fear took her by such force that the sudden desire to throw herself into his arms, crush him tightly to her, keep him with her forever washed over her. She swallowed hard and looked into his eyes.

Bill bent to kiss her, and the oddest feeling that it was a kiss of farewell—and not just for this moment—hit her. Sarah pushed aside her fears, refusing to give in to the weakness, but she did give in to the desire to embrace him more tightly, to kiss him with all the fervor she felt for him. His arms tightened around her, drawing her closer. After a while, he broke away from her lips and brought her head to rest against his chest and his wildly beating heart.

"If you keep that up, pretty Sarah, I might change my mind about letting you go." His voice was hoarse, half teasing. "Tomorrow evening, we'll be together again. You'll be back before you know it."

However, for all his best intentions, his words did nothing to reassure.

seventeen

"Please, sit down." Brent's voice was calm. "You make me uneasy just to watch you. You put me in mind of a prowling wildcat."

"Maybe it was a mistake letting her go." Bill plowed a hand through his hair and held the nape of his neck. "She's new to this kind of world, this kind of life. And Manhattan is so crowded."

"Sarah seems to be a woman of remarkable strength of character and high intelligence. I'm certain she'll do well."

"That city can be a zoo. I know. I lived there." Bill paced to the other end of the porch, then spun to face his brother. "The sharks she's accustomed to from her island are tame in comparison to the ones I ran into in that city. Though, granted, with the kind of company I kept, that was to be expected." He gave a mock-amused shake of his head.

"If you're so concerned, why did you change your mind and allow her to go?"

Bill expelled a long breath. "Just because I'm on a chain doesn't mean I want to keep her on a leash. I knew she wanted to go, and I knew she'd be safe in the men's care."

Brent sat back and took a drink of the lemonade beside him. "I must admit, the first time Darcy left with Charleigh to visit the city, I wasn't in complete favor of her going. Due to the fact that someone must remain behind with the boys, I haven't been able to partake of this particular event on any of the occasions they've visited the city, which amounts to three. Yet we've both found that the short absence from each other worked well for our marriage. It's helped us to appreciate each other that much more."

Bill couldn't even begin to relate. Six hours had elapsed since Sarah had left. They felt more like six weeks.

"However, you being so newly married, I imagine that what I said makes no sense to you at this moment."

Bill gave an amused snort. "You've got that right."

"Then neither do I need to ask if you've worked out your difficulties." Brent settled back in his chair. "Never mind. I've heard you whistling while you've been finishing work on the storehouse this past week, exactly as you did when we were boys. You only did that when everything was going well for you."

Needing to get his mind off of missing his wife, Bill looked out over the wooded horizon then back to his brother. "I noticed a chess set in the study. Would you be interested in a game after dinner? I imagine it's going to be awfully lonely around here without everyone." Without Sarah.

Brent laughed. "With fifteen boys for company? That's not likely."

"Yeah, you're probably right about that."

"A game does sound like a fine idea though." Brent stood. "But at this moment, I need to see about grading papers. And then I suppose I should check into what Darcy left us to eat. I know she made three roasts and four pies. Hopefully it will be enough to feed our army and provide sandwiches for lunch tomorrow."

Bill nodded, his appetite not that sharp. Once his brother retreated indoors, Bill took a seat on the top step of the porch. He'd worked harder than usual all day, trying to get his mind off the fact that his wife wasn't on the premises. The storehouse on which he, Samuel, and a few of the older boys were working was nearing completion.

Noticing that Sasi lay nearby, head on his paws in a dejected manner, his brown eyes sad, Bill reached over to scratch the pup between his ears.

"I know, little fella. I miss her, too."

Sarah's eyes went wide as she surveyed the island of Manhattan. When she had first arrived with Bill to New York, she had been exhausted, and the explosion of sight and sound had been too much to comprehend. Fully rested, it was still much to bear.

Building after building lined both sides of the street on which they stood, all of them tall, almost seeming to soar to the clouds. Horses and carriages intermingled with noisy automobiles. Hordes of people were everywhere—standing, walking, hurrying to catch a train.

Michael must have sensed her hesitation, for he patted her hand that she'd linked through his arm upon entering Pennsylvania Station. "There now, lass. 'Tis a sight to behold, to be sure. But there's no reason to fear. Stewart and I will be takin' good care of you, and that's the truth."

Sarah gave the old Irishman a grateful smile. Since they'd boarded the train hours ago and departed it, he had taken her under his wing, acting as a father toward her.

"Well, now that we're here, what shall we do first?" Ever the boisterous one, Darcy looked to and fro along the street, her eyes bright with excitement. The flower on her hat swung with the motions.

"Shall we get something to eat?" Charleigh asked Stewart.

"Now if you don't be mindin' it, I found a grand restaurant near the Italian district, serves the finest food in all the city." Michael's blue eyes twinkled. "That is, if ye don't mind the wait. I'd like to treat you."

"That sounds fine. But I need to speak with the judge before we do too much," Stewart said.

Darcy gave an affirmative nod. "After the apples I ate on the train, I can stand the wait."

"Don't forget the plums and peaches," Charleigh said with a wink.

"Can I help it if me appetite's increased now that I'm carryin' another wee babe?"

Charleigh grinned, though Sarah noticed the men looked uncomfortable with Darcy's reply. She assumed Darcy had spoken out of turn and said something she shouldn't, but then, "that was Darcy" as everyone was wont to say.

"I only hope the twins will be all right while I'm gone." Darcy looked pensive.

Charleigh squeezed her arm. "Brent has taken care of them on his own before. They'll be fine."

"Aye, but Beatrice is teething, and likely Robert Brent will be soon enough." She glanced at Clementine, who had looped one arm around her father's neck. "Perhaps I should 'ave brought both of 'em along."

Sarah listened to the two women, hoping she would be as good a mother as they were. Sometimes she had her qualms, but with each day, what Darcy called the mothering instinct grew more firmly planted within her.

"I suggest I drop you ladies off at the boutique, along with Michael; you do your shopping, make your orders; and we get something to eat then."

"Well, now, guv, I do like the sound of that," Darcy agreed.

"So do I." Charleigh nodded.

"Then it's settled." Stewart looked relieved

Sarah bustled along with the rest of them, and she couldn't help but notice, the men flanked either side of her, as if protecting her. She wondered if it was due to their promise to Bill to see to her care. The kindness all of them had shown her, "another odd egg," as Darcy liked to say, moved Sarah beyond words. She now felt as if she fit in with them, but she missed Bill. Tomorrow evening couldn't come soon enough.

An hour later at the boutique, she was shown a dress similar to the one she wore, though of a much darker color.

Darcy must have sensed her disappointment, for she turned to Mrs. Dempsey and shook her head.

"Nothin' doin'. This isn't for a funeral, after all. 'Aven't you got anything that doesn't look like it's the color of ashes from a pyre?"

The woman looked taken aback. "I had thought, what with Mrs. Thomas's condition, she would prefer something more sedate."

"She's carryin' a child, not a coffin."

"Co-ffin!" Clemmie squealed and clapped her hands.

Obviously flustered, the tall, rail-thin woman blinked and looked as if she might hyperventilate or pass out.

They had attracted the attention of another patron, a blond lady dressed in a beige chemise in the latest style. She wore a cloche hat snug to her head. A string of golden-orange beads circled her neck, reminding Sarah of the Pandanus seed necklaces she had made on the island. The woman looked at Sarah, then quickly averted her gaze.

Charleigh stepped in. "Perhaps something in a midnight blue?"

"Still too dark," Darcy insisted. "She needs somethin' bright and cheery. Like that lovely island dress she wore."

While Sarah left the women to decide the fate of her new dress, she watched the other woman, who edged closer to hear, though she kept her focus on the decor on the wall.

"The color red won't work, Darcy. All of Ithaca is bound to shun her then. You know that red is considered loose."

"I'm not sayin' to dress her as a floozy, Charleigh. I'm sayin' we might as well put her in somethin' Bill would like. What husband wants to see his wife in somethin' drab like that?" She nodded to the dress in question. "Might as well smear ashes on her forehead to give it the full effect."

"Bring us something yellow. Or pink," Darcy added to the boutique owner.

"Perhaps something in a muted shade of blue or green?" Charleigh suggested.

Mrs. Dempsey looked from one to the other throughout the entire exchange. She gave an uncertain vague smile and nodded before hurrying to disappear into a back room.

"Perhaps I was a mite hard on her?" Darcy asked.

"Perhaps just a bit." Charleigh grinned at Darcy's sheepish expression.

Sarah noticed the expensively dressed woman walk out the door of the boutique without having tried anything on. As she walked, she looked once through the window, meeting Sarah's stare, then hurried her pace until she was gone.

eighteen

A loud squalling from the blanket on the grass made both Bill and Brent jump.

"Here." Brent's tone was almost frantic as he thrust little Robert into Bill's hands. "You hold him. I need to see what's wrong with Beatrice."

"Wha—I can't. . ." But it was too late, and Bill sat holding his nephew like a sack of potatoes. He stared into the child's eyes. The boy looked at him a few seconds, then scrunched up his round face as if he was about to let loose with a bellow to match his sister's.

"Oh, no you don't." Feeling like a fish suddenly tossed onto dry land, Bill shot up from the chair, jiggling the baby up and down. Robert sniffled a bit, then opened his mouth wide and began to bawl.

"Hey, little fella." Desperate, Bill held the boy on his back, lying against one arm, as he'd seen Brent do. "You got a raw deal being stuck with me, didn't you?" He jiggled him again, only softer this time, and walked with him up and down the porch. Robert's cries lessened to a faint wail.

"Tell you what, you tell me your sob story, and one day your uncle Bill will tell you his. When you're much older, that is." The boy fully quieted. He hiccupped a couple of times and looked up at Bill, his sky-blue eyes wide as if he could understand.

"What, clamming up already?" Bill chuckled and lifted his hand to the side of Robert's head, stroking the baby fine hair with one finger for an instant. How did babies get to be so soft? "A little young to be worrying about spilling the beans, aren't you?"

"You do that well."

Bill looked at Brent in surprise. His brother walked up the porch stairs, Beatrice in his arms. The girl looked at Bill, then swung her tear-stained face away, burying it into Brent's neck.

"You would make a good father."

Brent's unexpected words of praise settled inside Bill and shook him at the same time. "Me? A good father?"

"Yes, you."

Bill considered Brent's words. The thought of creating a child with Sarah, of becoming a father to a helpless baby, boggled his mind. What kid would want to get stuck with him?

As though Brent could read his mind, he shook his head. "You don't give yourself enough credit, though in that regard I doubt I've been much aid to you. I was leery of you when you first came here; I admit it. Because of your criminal associations, a number of desirable positions in the teaching field were formerly closed to me. Stewart gave me an opportunity, and now looking back, I can see God's hand was upon that path of my life. Yet once I was bitter because you and I bore the same name and blood."

Uncertain of how to respond, Bill stared. This was the first he'd heard any of it. Shame caused him to lower his gaze to the porch, and he looked at the cracks there.

"Yet I would be remiss not to note that a different man came home than the one who left here more than a year ago. I've seen the changes; you're not the same person."

Bill looked up. The boy in his arms started to sniffle and shudder again, and Bill absently jiggled him.

"The truth of the matter is—and I say this with all sincerity—I'm happy to have you with us at the refuge. I'm relieved you came home." Brent's expression was earnest.

Tears stung Bill's eyes, and he had trouble swallowing over the lump in his throat. "Thanks for telling me."

As they stared at one another, the years, the obstacles, all fell away. Both men walked toward one another at the same time, closing the distance, and with their free arms, they embraced as brothers at long last.

❧

After being fitted in a dress that was a pleasant shade of blue and receiving two other dresses, one a fine dress of yellow linen for church meetings, and another in a rich shade of green with cream lace, Sarah felt speechless at the women's generosity.

"Posh," Darcy said. "You need it. And family takes care of family. Isn't that right, Charleigh?"

"Darcy's right." Charleigh gave Sarah a one-armed hug. "We may not be blood-related, but that doesn't make you any less family. Bill works for the refuge now, and you both live in our home. We take care of our own."

Afterward, Michael, who'd been waiting on a sofa provided for members of the male gender while their women tried on garments, rose to greet them. "Did ye find all ye needed?"

"Yes, Papa." Charleigh smiled at Sarah. "We chose some lovely dresses, and the seamstress assured us they would be ready to collect in the morning before our train leaves."

"Splendid. Then I suppose we should go meet Stewart. I imagine his meeting is long over."

They found Stewart at the aforementioned meeting place in Central Park, which to Sarah was like a haven of trees and grass in the midst of a stone and wood jungle. He looked at Charleigh, his manner somewhat tense. Without asking why, all eyes were drawn to the small child who sat on the bench beside him. Her face dirty, her brown hair in pigtails, she glared up at them. The apprehension that marked her face belied her tough exterior.

"Stewart?" Charleigh's eyes were wide as she turned to him.

He cleared his throat. "This is Miranda. She'll be joining us at the refuge."

Stunned silence met his announcement.

"A girl?" Charleigh blinked, looked back at the child, then at Stewart.

"See, I told ya they wouldn' want me." Miranda scowled and shot off the bench.

Still looking at Charleigh, Stewart caught the girl by the sleeve before she could go anywhere.

"Let me go! Get your stinkin' hands off me!"

"Judge Markston has handed Miranda over to my care," he explained, not looking at the girl. "Bill's almost finished with the storehouse. Perhaps it's time to make it official and take in girls as we talked about months ago. We could use the storehouse to house the older boys and give Miranda their room."

Charleigh shared a long look with him, then smiled. "Perhaps it is time at that. But oh, what will the townspeople say when they find out?" Her words were spoken lightly, and he chuckled. She looked at Miranda. "And we do want you. You are welcome."

Darcy moved forward and held out her hand. "Hello, Miranda. Me name's Darcy. I'm the cook there."

Miranda just glared.

"Well, I think I be hearing my stomach a-growlin'," Michael inserted. "Am I the only one ready to enjoy a meal?"

All in agreement, they hailed a cab, and soon the horse-drawn carriage brought them to their destination. They settled behind the red- and white-checked tablecloth of a fine-looking establishment. Sweet strains of music came from a far corner, and Sarah looked to see a dark-haired gentleman playing an instrument at one of the tables. Delicious aromas, such as she had never known, made Sarah's mouth water. Everyone at the table engaged in pleasant conversation. All except for the newcomer, Miranda. She sat in her chair, arms crossed over her chest, and pouted as if she were being jailed.

However, when a plate of what Darcy called spaghetti was placed before her, the child's eyes widened, and she leaned forward to practically inhale the long noodles and meatballs without waiting for the blessing Stewart gave.

Once they finished their meal, with Sarah now labeling Italian food a new favorite, a lovely young girl, not quite a woman, came to the table. Sarah stared at her curiously. This girl, with her long fair hair held back with a blue ribbon that matched her bright eyes, seemed different from the dark-haired workers Sarah had seen, among them the exotically beautiful older woman who'd served them their meal.

"Hello. My name is Melissa. My aunt Maria was called away suddenly, and she asked me to come and see if there's anything else you need. My aunt Maria and uncle Tony own this restaurant," she added proudly.

"It's a lovely place," Charleigh said. "I can't help but think that your aunt looks familiar, yet I've never been here before."

The girl gave a delicate shrug. "She rarely leaves the restaurant, so I don't know where you two might have met."

"Perhaps at the boutique?"

"It's a possibility." She looked toward the door as it opened and frowned. When she looked at them again, her smile had returned. "I need to go back to the kitchen now. On behalf of my uncle and my aunt, I want to thank you for visiting our establishment."

"It was a delight," Stewart assured. "The food was superb."

Melissa gave a faint smile and nod, again casting a distant glance toward the door before she hurried away.

Sarah turned to see what had captured the young girl's interest. A black-haired man in a sharp-looking three-piece suit with padded shoulders and wearing a fedora sauntered to a nearby table. A waiter suddenly appeared at his elbow, effusively greeting him.

Stewart also looked that way and frowned. "I think it's best we leave. I'm certain the women will want to freshen up at the hotel before the show tonight."

Charleigh looked his way, her brows drawn up in curiosity, to which Stewart only gave a slight quelling shake of his head. His eyes flicked to the man at the table, and Charleigh followed his gaze. She looked back at him, her eyes widening, and he gravely nodded.

Sarah didn't miss the signals between them. As they left, she directed a stare toward the mysterious man seated at the table. As if he felt her curiosity, he looked up at her. Sarah's heart iced over at the evil she sensed behind the man's dark eyes before he lowered his gaze back to the wine the waiter had brought him.

No one had to tell her why Stewart was suddenly so anxious to leave. Sarah had no doubt that she was staring at one of Vittorio's henchmen.

An uneasy pall covered the group, but the men later decided to go ahead and take the women to see the Ziegfeld Follies. Sarah enjoyed the music, the costumes, and the dancing considerably, no longer worried about Vittorio or his family. The restaurant was located on the other side of the city; the chances of them running into any of the men in this theater were slim. And as Michael and Stewart had reassured her earlier, the man didn't even know she was Bill's wife, so there was no reason for alarm.

All through the spectacular presentation, Darcy excitedly spoke under her breath to Sarah, who sat in the aisle seat. Charleigh had opted out, staying behind at the hotel with Clementine and Miranda, saying she'd seen plenty of Broadway shows and wanted Sarah to go and enjoy herself.

And she did. She enjoyed the colorful costumes, the pageantry, the music, but when she returned to her hotel room, it was with a sense of relief. Unaccustomed to the business and night life of such a bustling city, she looked forward to returning home to the countryside of the refuge tomorrow. And to Bill. She missed him so.

Clutching a second pillow to her chest, she lay on her side to sleep.

nineteen

"I don't like the looks of that sky." Bill stood on the porch late in the afternoon, hands on his hips as he stared at the dark cloud bank. "Soon it'll be raining pitchforks, unless I miss my guess."

"It certainly will make traveling to the station difficult, since I'll need to take the wagon as the automobile will not hold everyone." Brent surveyed him from the chair where he sat, holding both twins on his lap. "We still have only the one; the brake on the other vehicle isn't yet fixed."

Bill nodded. "It's an old hay-burner if you ask me. Too expensive to run," he clarified for Brent.

"I hope that the rain doesn't interfere with the picnic this coming weekend."

"Picnic?"

"Didn't I mention it earlier this week?" Brent shook his head. "Perhaps fatherhood makes one forgetful."

"You always did have your head in the clouds." Bill's comment lacked the mockery of old times but still bore a wealth of teasing. "Seriously, you're a good father, Brent. I've watched you these past two days, and it's been nothing short of amazing how you take care of those two. I don't know how you've managed as well as you have without Darcy here."

"The first occasion was difficult," Brent admitted as he rescued his spectacles from Robert's seeking hands, which had found Brent's pocket. "However, I learned by both experience and mistake. Darcy almost single-handedly tends to the children approximately 363 days of the year. Giving her a few days' reprieve to enjoy Manhattan twice in that same year

135

wasn't so much to offer. Though I must admit, had I known that both Beatrice and Robert were teething, I might not have been so eager to enlist my aid. I hope she didn't keep you awake all night?"

"Between her and Sasi's howling, it was an experience." Bill chuckled. The truth was that without Sarah beside him, he'd found it difficult to sleep. "About the picnic. . . ?"

"Ah, yes, the picnic. There will be a church picnic by the lake after the meeting this Sunday. It's an annual event before we must bid the summer farewell."

Robert suddenly began wailing. Bill moved toward his brother. "I'll take her if you need to see to Robert."

"Yes, thank you." Once Bill took Beatrice, Brent went with the boy into the house. He was back a few minutes later. "I don't like this. Robert seems to be running a temperature, likely due to teething, but I certainly don't want to take him outdoors due to the possibility of rain. Darcy would have my head if I exposed him. Would you mind terribly going to the station alone to collect them? You do remember how to get there?"

"After the turnoff, there's only one road to follow, Brent." Bill shook his head, amused. "I think I can find the place."

"Splendid."

Bill swiped his jaw, noticing the rough whiskers. "Maybe I'll head out early and get a trim and a shave while I'm at it."

"Ah, yes. You do want to get dolled up and look spiffy for Sarah. Of course, I do believe she already thinks you're the bee's knees." Brent's eyes twinkled.

Bill stared at his brother. "I don't believe it. Twice in almost two weeks with the slang. Be on the level with me. Are you an imposter? Have you kidnapped my brother?"

"I do believe it was bound to happen one day. I'm surrounded by slang, no matter what efforts I employ to try to train the boys to speak properly. And then, there's my wife."

He grinned. "It's difficult to maintain the quality of stuffiness in such exacting situations."

Bill laughed. It felt like old times again, when they were kids and used to josh each other and horse around. Since yesterday, Brent had completely let down his guard around Bill, bantering with him like he used to do when they were young boys, when Brent had looked up to Bill while Bill regarded him as his kid brother. Bill missed Sarah tremendously, yes, but at the same time he was thankful for this opportunity he'd had to share with Brent and really talk. The occasions had been rare in the past weeks, but once the boys were in bed last night, the two had found one another out on the porch and breached the chasm in their relationship.

"Well, I'm off. Toodle-oo!" Bill lifted a hand in a wave as he stepped off the stairs.

"Cheerio!" came the good-natured reply.

Bill shook his head in amusement without looking back. That one had to be Darcy's doing. Once again, he mentally tipped his hat toward her for teaching his brother to relax and enjoy life.

The drive into town went well—no rain. He headed to the barber shop, glad to see only one other customer there. A towel lay over his face, and his head rested back against the chair he sat in.

The barber, a plump man in his fifties, looked Bill's way. "I know you. You're Brent's brother—Bill Thomas. Right?"

"Yeah?" Bill waited.

"A man was in here an hour or so ago, looking for you."

"A man?" Bill thought a moment. Maybe the train was early, though that would be odd. Train schedules were very strict. "Did he give his name? Was it Stewart Lyons? Or Michael Larkin?"

"No, no. I know both of those gentlemen." As he spoke,

he moved a straight razor up and down a strop. "This was a stranger."

A stranger. Fear locked down hard on Bill. "What did he look like?"

"Blond gent. Medium height—about as tall as you. Blue eyes." His own eyes brightened. "He talked with a funny accent."

"It was French," came from behind the cloth of the man waiting for his shave.

"Yeah. That was it—French. Had that smooth ooh-la-la sound to it."

Bill stared. The man he described sounded just like Philip Rawlins, only he knew his old associate didn't work for Vittorio any longer. "Did he leave any kind of message?"

"No. Said he was just passing through town and heard you were here."

"Thanks." Forgetting all about his shave and haircut, Bill left the shop in a daze.

Why would Phil Rawlins search him out? Unless it wasn't Phil Rawlins at all, but one of Vittorio's hatchet men. . .no, that made no sense. The killers Vittorio had working for him in the family were mostly Italian; not blond with French accents.

Bill walked down the street, the minutes rambling by without order, while he tried to unscramble the situation in his mind. As he walked past the postal office, he noticed a dark-haired middle-aged woman who sat on a bench outside and fanned herself with a newspaper. She looked up at him as if she knew him.

"You're Bill Thomas? From Lyons' Refuge?"

"Yes."

"I thought so. I've seen you in church. I have something for you. A man came by and dropped it off. I'd put it with the other mail for the refuge, but as long as you're here, I'll go and get it. And you can have the rest of the mail, too."

This day was taking on a surreal aspect. "Thanks, I'd appreciate it."

Soon she waddled back out to the porch, a sheaf of envelopes and magazines in her hands. Bill took the bundle with another word of thanks and began walking away as he shuffled through the correspondence, a *Saturday Evening Post,* another few envelopes, a circular—until he found what he was looking for.

He stared hard at the plain envelope that bore his name and the name of the refuge underneath. Knowing he couldn't read it and juggle the rest of the items, he returned to the wagon, set the rest of the mail on the bench, and tore into the letter:

> *Bill,*
>   *Don't ask why I'm doing this or even how I know. Call it payback for saving my life like you did that time I put the bite on V and he planned to bump me off. For reasons I don't want to touch on here, I can't visit you at Lyons' Refuge, so I wrote this note instead. V knows you didn't die. A life for a life—that's always been his motto, and he won't stop until he finds you and makes that happen. You're no chump; take this as a warning. Keep your back covered. If I were you, I'd pack a rod at all times.*
>
> *P. R.*

So, it was Phil. The warning from his old associate wove deep down into Bill's mind, making him both angry and tense. He had gotten his life in order, was finally trying to stay on the up and up and do what was right. He'd brought God into his life—so why was this happening to him? Why now, when his relationship with Sarah was working out so well and they'd discovered mutual love? Sarah. . .

Horror swept through him.

A life for a life.

Closing his eyes, Bill felt the warning scream down into his very soul.

≈

Confused, Sarah studied her husband all through dinner. Since he had collected them at the station, she had sensed his unease. When he'd embraced her at the depot, he'd held her tightly for several seconds, almost as if he were afraid to let her go, then gave a faint, flippant smile when he pulled away. Even Stewart asked if anything was the matter, a question which Bill carelessly shrugged off with the comment that he'd missed his wife.

Sarah had missed him, too, but that didn't account for Bill's strange behavior. The troubled look she'd seen in his eyes all night. The heavy set to his shoulders as if they carried an unseen weight.

"Bill?" She came up to him where he sat on the porch, staring blankly at the stars. No one was with them, and he pulled her onto his lap. "What's biting you? You seem so worried." She pushed at a lock of his hair.

Despite his tense expression, he quietly chuckled. "If you're going to speak slang, pretty Sarah, you need to get it right. It's 'what's eating you?'" His words were gentle, teasing, but she didn't want to be put off.

"Please tell me," she quietly insisted.

He looked at her a long time, his eyes roving to each part of her face as though memorizing it.

"Bill?"

"Let's go away, Sarah. Just the two of us. We can find somewhere nice, somewhere quiet, safe. Build a life there."

"Go away?" Her brows pulled together in confusion. "Don't you like it here at the refuge? Now that you and your brother are getting along so well, I should think you would want to stay."

"It's all right here, I guess." He grew somber and looked into the distance. "There sure are a lot of kids around, though. And that new one has a mouth on her that won't quit. She'd shame a sailor."

Something twisted inside her heart. "You don't like kids, Bill?"

"Oh, I don't know." He seemed frustrated as he shook his head. "They're all right, I guess. But I think maybe we should head off somewhere else for a while. I hear Connecticut is nice. That's where your father is from if I remember right."

"Yes, he told me this. But why Connecticut? I have no relatives there any longer."

He blew out a heavy breath. "I don't know, Sarah. If you don't want to go there, that's fine. We can go somewhere else. I just want to get out of New York for a while."

She remained quiet as she observed him. She loved the refuge and all the people in it, who'd become her family. But she loved Bill more. "If you want to go to Connecticut, then we shall go. I only want for us to be together."

"Doll, you can't get rid of me."

The hoarseness in his voice confused her. He swallowed hard, and Sarah wondered in shock at the tears she saw glazing his eyes. But she had no time to think of his unpredictable behavior as his hand went to the back of her head and he swiftly pulled her toward him.

His mouth on hers both thrilled her and frightened her. He kissed her urgently, passionately, as if it were the last time he might ever do so. A maelstrom of emotion swept through Sarah at his kiss, and she kept her arms around his neck as if to hold on. With her answering kiss, she tried to show him her reassurance and her devotion, tried to comfort him and not be frightened.

But later that night, as Bill lay trembling in her arms, again holding her so very tightly, Sarah knew something was definitely wrong.

twenty

"I shall miss you." Charleigh helped Darcy with the dishes and looked toward Sarah. "At least you'll be coming with us on the picnic this weekend."

"Yes. Bill wanted to attend the church meeting once more and spend one last day with everyone here in a leisurely atmosphere." Sarah laid the plate she'd just dried onto a shelf. Feeling a fluttering inside similar to one she'd first felt on the night she lay in her hotel room in Manhattan, she put a hand to her stomach.

Darcy took her hands out of the dishwater and glanced Sarah's way, her expression concerned. "How are you feelin', luv? Is the sickness any better?"

"I'm doing much better. Only. . ." She hesitated, wondering if she should speak. Seeing only kindness in the women's eyes, feeling a closeness to them she'd never had with any other woman, including her aunt, she decided to share. "I have not yet told Bill about the baby. I fear he doesn't like children and I may lose him if he knows." Without warning, the tears came, and she buried her face in the dishtowel. She had been so emotional lately and couldn't seem to quench this latest outburst. Her shoulders shook as she tried.

She felt Darcy's arm slip around her waist as she drew her close. "There, there. Don't cry so." She smoothed her hair. "Bill loves you—even a blind man could see that. And I don't think he dislikes children neither. Brent told me he took quite a shine to Robert Brent. Held both babies in his arms and helped Brent take care of 'em while we was away. Poor dears. That's sayin' a lot for two teethin' babies!"

Sarah hiccupped softly and looked up. "Really?"

"Most certainly." Darcy nodded emphatically as if to prove her point.

Charleigh dried her hands. "Sarah, I understand your fears, but like Darcy, I agree that they aren't warranted. Any day you'll be showing, and I really think you need to tell Bill soon. I know Darcy told you of my experience in keeping news of Clementine from Stewart when I carried her, and let me assure you, if I could go back and redo the past, I would have told him the moment I knew. It could have saved us so much heartache and pain."

"If only we could go back and redo the past." Sarah sighed as another thought took hold. "I've made a great many mistakes; the greatest I believe was to cleave to the pagan teachings of my aunt. Something deep inside me felt uneasy even as I listened and attended the ceremonies, but when my father distanced himself from me after my mother died, I was lonely. I relied on my aunt to show me love and attention. I believed what she said, and even later, after my father told me differently, I would not listen."

"You were a small child when that happened." Shaking her head, Charleigh laid a comforting hand against Sarah's shoulder. "It wasn't your fault. Now that you've matured into an adult and have learned and know the truth, you're making a wise decision to abstain from island beliefs."

Sarah nodded, deciding she must also make another decision. "You are right in what you advise concerning Bill. Already I have felt life within my belly, and I know I cannot hide it from him any longer. I will tell him about the babe at the picnic." In a relaxed setting—surely this would be the best place to reveal such news.

"I'm tickled pink to hear it," Darcy said with a grin. "And I'm sure your pot and pan will be just as pleased." At Sarah's blank stare, Darcy added, "your husband, luv. That's me cockney slipping in, as you no doubt have heard many times before." She let out a delighted laugh.

Sarah grinned. Between Bill's American slang and Darcy's British cockney, her vocabulary had increased immensely over the past weeks.

A baby started crying, and another one soon joined in.

"Poor lambs. I best go see what's troublin' 'em now." Darcy left the kitchen. Charleigh and Sarah resumed their task of washing the dishes.

"In a pig's eye! And I don't have to tell you nothin'."

Both women jumped upon hearing Miranda's shout from outside. They hurried to the door.

Miranda stood, fists on her hips, leaning toward two boys Sarah recognized as Petey and Clint. Her braids were askew as always; her reddened face smudged with dirt.

"You're just a dumb girl," Petey shot back. "You don't know nothin' nohow."

"Says you! I'm smarter than all of you put together."

"If you're such a smarty-pants, whatcha doin' here?" Clint taunted. "You musta got caught to end up in this place. Watcha do—snitch a lollipop off a baby?"

The boys snickered.

"None of your beeswax!" Miranda said hotly. "You're both just a bunch of bozos!"

"Oh, yeah—well, so's your old man," Clint shot back.

Miranda flew at him, knocking him to the ground. She straddled him, her fist flying, but Charleigh flew off the porch and caught her arm before the girl could punch him in the nose. Sarah followed but stayed a distance behind.

"Stop it!" Charleigh commanded. "All of you. Clint and Petey, march right to Mr. Lyons's office—now! Miranda, you come with me."

"Whatcha gonna do? Beat me to a pulp?" The girl glared at both women. "I ain't afraid of any of you."

Charleigh maintained calm. "Miranda, we would never strike a child in anger; that's simply not right, nor is it how we do things here at the refuge. But you will be disciplined. I cannot allow fighting to go unpunished. For now, I want you to sit on the porch. Do not move from that spot. I need to talk this over with Mr. Lyons."

Miranda wrenched her arm away from Charleigh and marched to the porch. With a huff, she flopped onto it, her skirts ruffling with the action. Sarah was surprised the girl had given in so quickly. Over the past several days at the refuge, she had rejected authority, though the second time she'd been sent to her room without supper. Perhaps that had helped to curb her rebellion.

Charleigh shook her head, the look she gave Sarah filled with concerned exasperation. "Would you mind keeping an eye on her while I talk with Stewart? She appears to have settled down some, but I'd prefer it if she wasn't alone."

"Of course."

Charleigh left for the house. Sasi, who'd awoken from his nap, came to sniff Miranda. The girl put out her hand and tentatively petted the pup. Seeing Sarah approach, she quickly withdrew her hand.

"You may pet Sasi if you like." Sarah smiled, but the girl looked away. She hesitated, then sat on the porch, keeping Sasi between them. Sasi moved to lick Sarah's hand, and she absently petted the puppy. He playfully nipped at her, and Sarah chuckled.

"Is he yours?" Miranda asked, still staring straight ahead.

Sarah sensed a strange longing in the child's voice. "Yes. My husband gave him to me. I've always had a great fondness for animals. On the island where I was born, I had a pet monkey and a dolphin."

Miranda turned wide eyes to Sarah. "No foolin'? I seed pictures of 'em in books before, but never seen one in real life. My pa wouldn't let me have a dog. Wouldn't let me have nothin'. Exceptin' the back of his belt." The girl turned sullen again.

Wanting to bring back the shine she'd seen in Miranda's eyes, Sarah spoke. "I suppose I truly did not own either of them. They were wild and only came to visit me when they were ready. I miss them, but now I have Sasi." She reached down to rub his belly, and Sasi's tail thumped the porch. "The monkey was actually a gift to my father, but he did not like Mutu. He would often steal his bananas or other fruit from him when my father was not looking. He never did so to me, though. We had an understanding. I carried him through the forest, and he did not steal from my plate." Sarah grinned and was pleased when Miranda smiled. But again it faded.

"Sometimes if you wanna eat ya gotta steal," the girl countered in sad resignation. "Ain't nothin' you can do about that."

Sarah thought a moment. "You should talk to Darcy. When she was a girl, she lived in the streets of London and stole food to eat. She was also a pickpocket. She stole money from gentlemen's pockets."

Miranda's eyes widened. "Really? I figured she was just a goody-goody like the rest of 'em."

"Goody-goody? I have not heard this term."

Miranda gave a scornful half laugh. "Lady, you are way behind the times. A goody-goody is someone who's too good to be true. Like this place." She shook her head. "Ain't no way these people here are real. One day I'm gonna wake up and they'll be just as mean as my pa was."

Sarah felt saddened by the girl's pain. "And your mother?"

"She ran off long ago. Who needs her anyway?" Scowling, Miranda picked up a pebble lying nearby and threw it far across the lawn.

"I also had no mother. I lost her when I was seven."

Miranda looked at Sarah. "That's when my old lady ran out on me. Two years ago. Pa's been meaner than a hornet ever since, though he took off, too. Took his money and gambled it all away."

Sarah stared out over the lawn as silence settled between them. Something inside urged her to speak. "This term, *goody-goody*. It makes me think of God, and how He is all that is good. My father taught me that no one is truly good, and that is so. Everyone at one time or another does what is wrong when they wish to do what is right. The people here at the refuge have God living inside their hearts; that is the goodness you see. They want to reach out and share this goodness with others. Everyone here has been through many difficulties, as you have. Charleigh served a term in a British prison for her crimes, as did Darcy. That is where they met."

Shock covered Miranda's face. "No foolin'?"

Sarah nodded. "They would not mind me speaking of this, since everyone here knows of their story. Do not be afraid of this goodness you see, Miranda. It is real and will not be taken from you."

Miranda looked away and didn't answer. Seconds elapsed before she turned to Sarah again. Her eyes seemed hopeful, though hesitant. "Will you tell me more about your dolphin and your monkey?"

Sarah laughed, grateful that Miranda had finally reached out. "I would be most honored to."

ða

Stewart's eyes were grave as he set the letter on the desk. He looked up at Bill. "Why should Eric do this, is what I want to know? What kind of hidden motive does he have?"

A tap sounded on the door, and Charleigh walked inside. "Oh, sorry to interrupt. I'll come back later."

"No, wait." Stewart looked at Bill then back to his wife. "You need to hear this, too."

Curiosity lifting her brows, Charleigh approached the desk. Stewart handed her the letter. She read over it, then looked up, her eyes even more confused.

"P. R. is Philip Rawlins. . .Eric."

Her face blanched. Stewart rose from his chair to put an arm around her shoulders. "Don't worry, sweetheart. I won't let him near you again."

She nodded faintly, then looked at Bill. "Is this why you feel you must leave the refuge?"

The refuge. An odd choice of words. Was anywhere really safe?

"It would be best for everyone here if we did leave. And please, I don't want Sarah to know about that letter."

"You don't want your wife to know a killer might be after you?" Stewart shook his head. "Is that fair to her? Don't you think she should be told?"

Bill wondered about that. If he thought that it was only about him, he might be able to handle the prospect of Vittorio's henchmen lurking somewhere close by far better. But the fear that Sarah was the target had him literally trembling. Ever since he'd received the missive, Bill was frantic, his emotions so near the surface he'd been unable to control them or hide them from his wife. That had been the motivation for him bringing the letter to Stewart. He hoped somehow Stewart could help him.

"You can't run all your life, Bill." Stewart's words were calm. "After Connecticut, then where? There will always be some place else you'll feel the need to run. The offer to stay here with Sarah still stands."

Frustrated, Bill shook his head, rubbed a hand along his nape. "You don't know these people like I do. What Phil wrote—a life for a life—is exactly how Vittorio thinks. He won't stop until he achieves his purpose. Phil knows that, too."

He noticed the look they shared.

"Look, I know you don't think much of Phil—or Eric, as you knew him," Bill corrected. "But he was my friend; I saved his life once, and that means something in the underworld where I come from. I don't think he's playing me for a sap. This is on the level. And I also think if he meant you guys harm, he wouldn't have written that letter. He would have come here. He didn't try to disguise the fact that it was from him."

"You could be right about that." Stewart's answer was grim. "Still, I'd find it hard to believe that there was any morsel of good in the man."

Charleigh put a gentling hand to Stewart's tense arm, and he relaxed, again glancing at her. His gaze softened.

Bill could understand their dilemma. He'd heard everything his former associate had done to this poor woman. Deceiving her into believing they were married, using her as his fellow con-artist, and then, after the *Titanic* sank, searching her out and threatening her again. His own brother had saved everyone at the refuge on the night Phil had arrived to wreak his revenge. But Bill would be a sorry soul if he were to judge Phil for his past sins when his own were just as bad.

"If I were packing heat, I'd feel safer, but I no longer have a gun."

"I'm sorry. I have no gun to give you. Here at the refuge, especially considering some of the situations these children come from, we find it safer not to have firearms on the premises. But I do understand your dilemma, and I'm not suggesting that it isn't real. I believe it's very real."

"The only protection I can offer you is my prayers," Charleigh said earnestly. "You and Sarah will always have those."

"Yeah, thanks." Bill tightened inside. If God really cared about his life, would He have allowed this to happen? He'd asked God to take over, but Bill figured somewhere along the line, God must have gotten lost, too. He didn't understand this alarming course on which he was being taken.

As if he'd read his mind, Stewart eyed him somberly. "Sometimes, even after we become Christians, we end up having to suffer the consequences for past mistakes. Maybe it doesn't seem fair, and maybe it doesn't seem like God really cares. But He does. And we just have to keep trusting Him to work out our lives, even when it seems like everything is falling apart."

Bill nodded, knowing Stewart was just trying to help, though he wasn't sure he bought all of what the man said. He'd be happy when he and Sarah were out of New York.

twenty-one

"We'll be leaving for the picnic as soon as the twins are up from their nap."

Sitting on the edge of the bed, Sarah nodded and continued staring at the object in her hand. As she studied the last few engraved symbols, Bill came to sit beside her.

"Your father's cross?" he asked, and again she nodded. "Do you understand what all those symbols mean?"

"Most of them." She explained to him that the wavy lines meant the prayers of her father, and then enlightened him to the other symbols she'd figured out. Afterward she motioned to the top of the last two. "This, I think, means you." She pointed to a symbol next to the crown. "When Maliu brought you to the island and I found you."

Bill leaned forward to see, then snorted. "Please tell me that's not what I think it is."

Sarah's smile grew wide. "Yes, it is an angel. My father was very fond of the meanings of symbols and names and studied them. The night before we married, he told me that your true name—William—means *determined guardian*. Like an angel, perhaps?" Her heart fairly danced as he shook his head in embarrassed agitation.

"Why is it carrying that crown?"

"The crown is me. The name Sarah means *princess*. You, my guardian, carried the princess away from the island."

His eyes clouded over. "Do you regret that, Sarah? I've sometimes wondered if you held it against me."

"No, Bill. I have found much happiness with you here in New York. More than I ever dreamed possible. I wouldn't have left the island with you had I not wanted to."

They shared a tender look, and he pointed to the bottom symbol. "What's that last one mean?"

Sarah again studied the symbol that had given her so much confusion. The crown was closed off inside a thick circle and separate from the symbols on the outside, which were at opposite angles. A snake. A cross. "This one I do not know. I have studied it and studied it. The snake, I think, means evil, and the cross is good. Perhaps showing that Aunt Lefu's way was evil and Father's way was good?" She shook her head. "But why it shows at the bottom is what I don't understand."

Bill intently looked at the carving a long moment. "Sarah, what if this was your father's way of showing you that you had closed yourself within two worlds and must make a choice? That you can't serve more than one God?"

At his quiet words, a flash of blinding clarity streamed through her mind. Her father had tried to talk to her several times after his great sorrow when he had returned to God to point out that Sarah shouldn't attend the pagan ceremonies or cleave to the words of her aunt. But she hadn't understood since he'd never stopped her before. And so he had discontinued his counsel. Was this his last way of reaching out to her, to try and get her to realize the truth?

Tears swam to her eyes as she looked at Bill. "I think you may be right. I think that must have been the message that Father was trying to tell me. If only he could know that I've learned the truth and now in my heart serve only one God. The true God."

With his index finger, Bill traced one of the wavy lines. "I think he probably does know, Sarah."

&

A balmy breeze heightened the summer day, making it comfortable. Bill joined Sarah on the blanket for their picnic. With them, Darcy and Brent, Charleigh and Stewart, all enjoyed sandwiches while the children played, having already engulfed their food. Their excitement over running through the grass or wading in the lake nearby made everyone smile. Even Miranda seemed to be enjoying herself and didn't pick fights with the boys as she often did.

Robert Brent crawled over to Bill, grabbed his index finger, and put it in his mouth, gumming down on it.

Darcy tugged on his diaper, pulling the boy back. "Now then, you'll not be usin' people for teethers, young man."

"That's all right." Bill gave a smile of consent, then looked down at the kid. "Me and Robert have an understanding, don't we, little fella?"

Robert made gurgling noises as he continued to gum Bill's finger. Bill looked up at Sarah and was stunned by the glow of happiness in her eyes. "Sarah?" he breathed in confusion.

She looked down at her lap, but he couldn't miss the shyness that swept over her face. Darcy and Charleigh exchanged a grin.

"Well now, as much as we'd love to keep your company, bein' as how ye will soon be leavin' the refuge, I think it's a splendid day for young lovers to take a walk." When neither Bill nor Sarah made a move, Darcy shooed them. "Do I need to set a fire underneath you? Well then, off with ye both."

Brent chuckled. "Trust me, Bill. You'd be wise to just do as she suggests."

"I like the idea." Stewart rose and held his hand out to Charleigh. "Shall we?"

She nodded, her eyes bright as she stood to take his arm, and the two began to walk. Bill and Sarah did the same, taking the opposite direction.

They hadn't gone far, when they heard the unmistakable sound of Sasi's yipping. Bill turned to look, and noticed Miranda following them and carrying the pup.

"Don't you have anything better to do?" Bill pointedly

asked. "I hear the children are going to have a potato-sack race soon."

"Don't like races."

"Well, then go take a swim."

"Can't. Don't know how."

Bill let out a frustrated breath. "Well, I'm sure you can find something to do rather than spy on your elders. In other words—scram!"

"Aw, no need to get in a lather, mister." Miranda scowled. "I know when I ain't wanted." She turned on her heel in a huff.

"Bill." Sarah put a hand to his sleeve.

"Can't a man spend time alone with his wife?" he implored, half amused, half frustrated.

"Yes, of course. But I think you were too hard on her. She has been through so much, and we have talked. I think she is starting to open up with me."

Bill looked into Sarah's gentle eyes, which always seemed to have the power to transform him from a growling bear to a bear cub within seconds. He blew out a resigned breath. "Yeah, maybe you're right. I was too hard on the kid. I'm just not used to them is all. Never been around any before I came to the refuge."

They continued walking and entered a shady area where the trees blocked them from view of the rest of the picnickers. Holding her hand, Bill led Sarah farther into the woods, then turned with a smile and pulled her into his arms for a long, tender kiss.

Caught up in the delight of Sarah, he heard the rustle of the grass only when it was too late.

"Well, now. Looks to me like Lucky Bill ain't so lucky after all."

An ominous click sounded.

Bill tensed and hurriedly pulled away from Sarah, setting her behind him so that he mostly stood in front of her.

In pinstriped suits and wearing fedoras, two men Bill recognized as Alfonzo and Lucio both pointed guns at Bill's heart.

❧

Fear tore into Sarah's mind. Dread ripped away her composure.

"Good thing Vonnie was at the boutique the day your little wife was," the darker of the two said.

Sarah recognized him as the stranger from the restaurant, and she clutched the sleeve of Bill's suit coat, her eyes wide. She realized these must be the mobsters Bill had been running from.

"You got what you want." Bill's voice was tight but calm. "Let her go."

His words of defeat terrified Sarah. She shot a glance to her husband, her grip on his arm tightening as if by force of will she could protect him from these men's evil intentions with her touch alone.

"Well now," the first man responded, "we can't do that, Bill. We don't need her running off to squeal. Besides, two for the price of one—Vittorio might like that." He raised his brows to his partner, who gave an unpleasant grin.

Bill tensed. "That's not Vittorio's way and you know it. She has nothing to do with any of this."

"What makes you think I care? She's just a dame. They're a dime a dozen as far as I'm concerned." The first man's dark eyes were cold. "Now. . ." He motioned with his gun for them to walk ahead of him. "It's time for you to take a little ride that's been long in coming. You, too, sister."

"You wanna find the real killer?" Bill stood his ground. "Tell Vittorio to take a good look at the Ferrelli family. I didn't kill Marco. I saved the man's life once; why would I kill him? I had no motive."

"Aw, go tell it to Sweeny."

"I'm not asking you to believe it, Alfonzo. I'm asking you to take me to Vittorio."

Sarah's heart froze. What was Bill doing? Vittorio would kill him before Bill ever opened his mouth; he'd told her so.

"He sent us to do the job." Alfonzo slightly waved his gun in a brisk movement. "You're trying my patience. Whether we do it here or somewhere outta the ways makes no difference to me. By the time those other picnickers get here, we'll be long gone."

Sasi's sudden barking startled them. Distracted, Alfonzo swung his head in that direction as the pup raced for him and grabbed a bite of his trousers hem. Sarah watched the other man aim at Bill and his finger move slowly on the trigger. She didn't stop to think, didn't stop to question. With all her strength, she pushed Bill out of the way.

In the next split second, the other man fired. Blinding pain tore through Sarah's side. A haze covered her eyes. The last thing she heard before sliding to the ground was Bill's panicked cry of her name.

twenty-two

Before Vittorio's men could fire again, Bill rushed to his wife's side, grabbing her upper body close to him. Red soaked her yellow dress and spread onto his shirt.

"No, Sarah! No! Dear God, why?" His cries were tortured. *"Why?"*

A loud rustling stirred the bushes. Men's voices could be heard. "Bill?" Stewart called.

"Someone's coming," Lucio said. "More than one. Sounds like an army."

"Let's scram!"

The two mobsters ran off before a large group of men hurried into sight.

Bill heard exclamations of horror and surprise. Someone called out to go and get the doctor. Bill felt someone else take hold of his arm.

"Bill," Brent said urgently but quietly, "we need to get her back to the refuge."

He looked up, dazed.

"No, that's too far away," a woman said. "Bring her to my house. It's closer."

The need for immediate action pushed shock into a temporary corner of Bill's mind. One of the men moved forward to help pick Sarah up, but Bill shook his head to stop him. He scooped Sarah up into his arms and held her close. Her head lolled to the side like a broken doll's.

Throughout the next hour, Bill learned what unending torment felt like. While the doctor remained with Sarah beyond a closed door, Bill was made to wait in the parlor of the woman who'd offered her home. He dully noticed she was one of those who'd always snubbed Sarah. Bill didn't even know her name, didn't want to know. All the faces and voices formed a blur in this nightmare world into which he'd been thrust. All he wanted was Sarah, alive, well. . . .

He numbly heard Stewart's explanation of how Miranda had followed the two, seen the mobsters, and run to get help. If it hadn't been for her, they'd both be dead. At this point, Bill didn't want to live if it meant Sarah must die. That bullet should have been his.

What seemed like eternities passed as Bill waited. Darcy and Brent tried to encourage him, offering comfort. Charleigh and Stewart did the same, as did Pastor Wilkins. But Bill knew no comfort, didn't deserve it. His former criminal actions had done this. He alone was responsible.

Why did she push him out of the way? Why did she do that?

The question tormented his mind.

When the doctor finally entered the parlor, his face was grave. Bill's heart fell into a deep hole as he stood up to hear the words that he didn't want to hear but must.

"I successfully removed the bullet, but she shouldn't be moved." The elderly doctor patted his brow and beard with a handkerchief. "If she pulls through the night, there's a good chance she'll make it. I'm sorry, but that's all I can give you."

Bill curtly nodded, his throat so tight he couldn't speak.

"I wasn't able to save the baby. I'm very sorry."

Baby?

Bill stared, shock rooting him in place and fogging his mind. "Sarah was pregnant?" His words were hoarse.

"You didn't know?" The doctor seemed surprised, then averted his gaze as if uneasy.

Bill drew on every remnant of control he possessed. "May I see my wife?"

"Of course."

Bill entered the darkened room, closing the door behind him. Sarah lay upon the white sheets, her skin pale, her eyes closed as if she merely slept. A sheet covered her slight form to her bare shoulders. She looked like an angel. The thought terrified him.

He dropped down on one knee beside the bed. Gently, he laid his hand over her small one. "Oh, Sarah, forgive me. . . . Please forgive me." Hot tears clouded his eyes and rolled down his cheeks. He lowered his head to her arm, hoarsely repeating the words of contrition in a mindless chant. Minutes passed.

All that mattered now was that she live. . . . *Please, dear God, let her live.*

Bill straightened and looked at her as if to memorize her face. With his fingertips, he tenderly traced the graceful line of her cheek, her jaw. "Pretty Sarah, open your eyes; don't leave me. You can't leave me. I don't want to go on living without you." He pressed his lips gently to the corner of her still ones. A tear dripped onto her cheek. "You must live, sweetheart."

Seeing her beautiful hair imprisoned in the thick braid frustrated him. His hands trembling, he unwove the long silky strands, freeing them and spreading them to one side of her in a shimmering curtain. His gaze went to her flat stomach, and at the reminder, another stab of pain sliced through him. She must have known for months.

"Why didn't you tell me about the baby, Sarah? Did you think I wouldn't want it?" Gently he brushed tendrils of her hair from her temple. Memory of those occasions she'd asked if he liked children and seemed apprehensive about his offhand responses accused him. These past nights, when they'd discovered their love and she'd lain in his arms, he'd felt the slight swell of her stomach but thought it was weight gained due to her renewed appetite for food. What a fool he was!

He closed his eyes. "Oh, Sarah, Sarah. God willing, we'll create another baby. I do want children with you. Just please, don't die."

Time passed, but Bill remained. Brent came inside and laid a consoling hand to his shoulder, trying to urge him away from the bedside to eat something. Bill refused, and Brent finally left him alone to his tortured vigil. Night darkened the windowpane.

Throughout the bleak hours, Bill sat near her bed and replayed every sin, every crime he'd ever committed. That his Sarah should have been the one to suffer for all of them sliced through his conscience, tore through his heart. Why couldn't it be him lying there? He deserved it. Why couldn't it have been him?

He watched her face, took note of the shallow rise and fall of her chest, afraid to look away, as if by staring at her he could keep her alive. His prayers were without words but contained his entire soul. If she did come back to him, he would never again fail to tell her of his love for her, would tell it to her a hundred times a day.

Early into the morning, exhaustion overtook him, and he laid his head down beside her arm to rest. Her moan woke him what could have been minutes or hours later. Snatched from uneasy sleep, he raised his head in shock. Saw her lashes flicker. His heart skipped erratically as she slowly opened her eyes.

"Bill. . ." Her word was a mere breath.

"I'm here, baby." Tears threatened again, and he squeezed her hand tightly. "I'm here. Just hold on; don't leave me. You're going to get well, and we're going to have a great life together. I promise."

In the depths of her dark eyes shone a look of such intense love it took Bill's breath away. She nodded her head slightly against the pillow in confirmation and again closed her eyes.

How could he have ever doubted her love for him? Never again would he.

He waited until he was assured Sarah slept peacefully, then rose, his legs numb and shaky from sitting for so long. Brent met him when he came outside the door. A wave of gratitude that his brother had been with him throughout the whole night threatened Bill's dubious composure. Relief caused everything to converge upon him at once.

"Bill?"

"I feel she's going to make it."

"I'm relieved to know it." Brent looked uneasy. "Do you think we should ask for the police to post a guard on the event that those men will return?"

Averting his gaze from his brother to the gray light now coloring the window, Bill swallowed hard over the grief that clogged his throat and stared straight ahead.

"Bill?"

"There's no need for that. A life for a life." Bill gravely looked at his brother. "Vittorio won't be bothering us again."

Without another word, Bill strode from the house. He kept walking until his legs burned, until his breath came fast and he could go no farther. Slumping down against a tree, he finally allowed the emotion to overtake him and wept for Sarah and the child he would never know.

twenty-three

Bill sat and stared at the cracks in the porch. He heard some-one come up beside him but didn't turn to look. For a long time, they remained silent.

"You need to stop taking all the blame," Charleigh said. "It wasn't your fault."

"How can you say that?" Head hung low, Bill threaded his fingers through his hair to the back of his scalp. "It was *only* my fault. If I hadn't joined up with those men years ago, none of this would have happened."

"Bill." She put a kind hand to his shoulder. "You simply can't go on like this. You haven't eaten, haven't slept. Forgive me for saying so, but you look terrible. You spend almost all your time sitting out here, staring at nothing. It's been almost three weeks. The doctor says Sarah's going to be fine. But she needs you to be strong right now; this has been very hard on her."

Bill swallowed hard. "How, Charleigh? How can I be strong for her when I feel as if my own soul and heart are crushed, when I know that all this happened because of me?" He looked at her, pleading. "Please. Tell me. How?"

She sank to the chair beside him, her manner one of gentle earnestness. "Only God can help you get through this, Bill. I know you're having a hard time trusting Him right now; I understand that. But you need to let go of the blame and stop looking at what you could have done differently in the past. We all make mistakes; we're human. Sometimes, unfortunately, we end up having to pay for those mistakes, as Stewart already told you. Even after we get right with God.

But what's important is to continue the course, to put this all behind you, and go on."

"Put it all behind me?" Bill stared at her, incredulous. "We lost a child. My wife was shot and almost died."

"I know." Her eyes were full of sympathy. "And I know what I'm saying doesn't seem to make sense right now, but it really is the way not only to survive but to live a life of victory. The days will get better; I speak from experience. When you accept Jesus into your life, the storms do come, but so do the blessings. And they will come for both you and Sarah. Just don't give up on God."

She hesitated, as if unsure she should speak. "What Sarah did in pushing you out of the way and then taking that bullet reminds me of the love God showed for us, in that He took the punishment that should have been ours. I really think you've punished yourself long enough, Bill. God forgave you. He died on the cross for you. Sarah forgave you, too."

Bill closed his eyes at that, emotion causing his throat to ache. Sarah had been nothing but gentle and loving, forgiving all his wrongs both past and present when he didn't deserve her forgiveness. In the cemetery now lay a small granite marker, an eternal testimony of his past sins, but she had never blamed him for the loss of their child or for any of his mistakes. And that sharpened his guilt almost to a point beyond what he could bear. He'd hardly been able to look at or be with her. Though it was all he wanted.

"Go to her. She needs you."

Bill nodded, resigned. He needed her, too, but still felt unworthy of her. He stood and went into the house, heaviness underlining his every step as he ascended the stairs.

When he opened their bedroom door, Sarah turned from the pillows to look at him. Such joy, such hope shone across her face and in her eyes, making Bill catch his breath. Gone were the days when she shielded her emotions; each nuance of expression told of her strong love for him.

"Sarah." Apprehension lifted from him as he quickly strode toward the bed and sat beside her, pulling her into his arms. Her head rested beneath his chin, and he fought the tears that now so often dwelled just beneath the surface. "I'm so sorry."

"Bill." Her hand reached up to press against his cheek, and she moved back as though to look at him. He stiffened his hold, not wanting her to see his tears. Regardless, they dripped onto her fingers.

"You have nothing to be sorry about," she said softly. "We have both suffered this loss. You aren't to blame."

He closed his eyes tightly. Would he ever believe that?

"I have felt so alone," she admitted. "Please don't go from me, too."

Her fearful tone sliced his heart, and he pulled away slightly, lifting his hands to cup her face. "Sarah, I will never leave you. Never. I've just been so confused, so upset. I didn't know how to sort out all that's happened to us. I still don't."

She nodded as though she understood. Tears ran from their eyes. They looked at one another seconds longer before he again drew her close. Weeping in each other's arms, they shared the pain of their loss.

While wrapped in one another's embrace, they experienced healing's first touch.

≈

"Sarah?"

At Bill's voice, she turned from entering the lake.

"I thought I'd find you here." He wrapped his arms around her waist in greeting and kissed her firmly. Pulling back, he gently slid a fragrant red blossom above her ear.

Sarah's heart leapt at his touch and his smile. Often he brought her roses in full bloom, since he'd told her about love's gentle fragrance. The continual bloom of their love filled her heart with song.

"Swim with me?" she asked.

He looked out at the lake. "Oh, well, why not?" He went to sit down and took off his shoes and socks. "The water shouldn't be too cold for early summer. At least I hope it isn't."

She giggled and pulled on his hand. "I have found that the cold can be invigorating."

The water was more than cold; it was frigid. Bill yelped and tried to shoot out of the lake, but Sarah tugged on his hand, pulling him in farther. "Do not cast a kitten or be such a high hat," she teased.

"Have a fit? Me? And pretty Sarah. . ." He changed his tactics, playing the predator to her prey. A flame kindled in his eyes, and his brows lifted with promise of sure retribution as he advanced a step toward her. "If you're going to call me a snob, then you'd better be willing to pay the consequences."

Squealing, she released his hand and splashed farther out until the water hit above her shoulders. He made a shallow dive after her. She didn't try very hard to escape, anticipating the moment of his sure victory.

He caught her and held her close. She melted against him. Soon neither of them felt the chill as he exacted his sweet revenge and she delighted in her defeat.

"I love you, Sarah," he whispered against her mouth long moments later. He pulled away to look into her eyes. "Every day that passes, I thank God that we're together. I hate what Vittorio did to us, but strange as it may sound, I think it bonded us even more. I never fully realized the extent of your love for me, or mine for you, until that day you took the bullet that should have been mine."

Sarah was surprised by his words. During her recovery all through the long fall and winter, and even into the spring, they hadn't spoken of that horrible day except briefly. Always, they tried to step around the subject that had brought them so much grief and loss.

She pressed her hand against his cheek. "I did not think; I only acted. I was afraid you would be killed."

"I almost did die when I heard that gun go off and saw you lying there."

Sarah remembered the pain, the heartache, the loss. Yet with Bill's love and encouragement, his tender care and touch, he had pulled her through that trying time, helping her to heal both in heart and in body. And she had helped him to heal as well. Together, they'd helped one another.

At first, fearful uncertainty that the men might return had tormented her, but Bill assured her that Vittorio had taken his vengeance. Bill knew these men, and he knew they would have observed from the shadows, learned of the private funeral, and would have looked to see the child's grave.

As though sensing her sudden melancholy, he tilted her chin so that she was looking into his turquoise-colored eyes. They gleamed with assurance, reminding her of inviting waters. "Don't be sad, pretty Sarah. We'll have a family some day. Whenever God thinks the time is right, we'll create another baby."

A slow smile tilted her lips. She took hold of his hand beneath the water and guided it to her flat stomach, pressing it there.

"The time is right."

Bill's eyes widened at her quiet words and he stared for a few seconds before he spoke. "You don't mean. . ."

"Yes."

"Are you sure?"

She nodded. "I am."

Bill's boyish whoops and hollers made Sarah laugh in delight. Their joy rang out over all the lake. Scooping her up into his arms, he held her close, while she wrapped her arms about his neck.

"I love you, Bill."

"And I love you, my pretty Sarah, always and forever."

She met his kiss, revealing all the feelings she had for him, never again holding back. For in both God's love and Bill's, she had found her source of true strength.

epilogue

Bill paced up and down the parlor. Outside, a wet snow fell. Each time he heard the creak of stairs, he halted his trek to dart a glance that way, but it was always only another of the children.

"Keep this up, guv, and we'll have to ship you off to Bedlam. I declare you must be wearing a hole in that rug." Darcy bounced her and Brent's newest baby, Madeline, over her shoulder. From the swell of her stomach, she would be expecting another child early in the summer. As would Charleigh, who walked in from the kitchen, bearing a huge pot of steaming water and towels over her arm.

"Let me get that for you, sweetheart." Stewart grabbed the pot and followed her upstairs. Bill noticed that since hearing news of the baby, Stewart had treated Charleigh like china, barely allowing her to lift anything at all. Much as Bill had treated Sarah.

"I don't recall ever seeing you this nervous about anything." Brent eyed Bill.

He threw his brother a disgusted look. "Don't you think the situation warrants it?"

Brent had the audacity to chuckle and settle back on the sofa, one of the twins sitting on each side of him. Clementine sat beside Beatrice, and both toddlers looked at the pictures in a book spread out on their legs. On the phonograph in the next room, Joel and Jimmy had put on a record that scratched out the tune "Ain't We Got Fun?"

Bill thought it highly inappropriate for the moment. Fun was the last thing he was having.

"Ah, but I've been through this event twice before, Bill. Truly, there's nothing to worry about."

"Aw now, guv'ner," Darcy teased as she came up behind him and laid a hand on his shoulder. "The way I heard tell it, you passed out cold when Robert Brent was born. Fainted dead away, he did." She winked at Bill in amusement.

"Yes, my dear. But Robert's presence was highly unexpected. I didn't know we were having twins."

Bill suddenly felt sick and dizzy at the same time. He'd heard twins ran in families. . .and Brent was his brother. The thought of having one was both terrifying and wonderful. The thought of two. . .

Suddenly from upstairs, the sound of a baby's lusty cry stopped everyone from what they were doing and had them glancing toward the ceiling.

Brent's smile widened as he looked at Bill. "Congratulations, big brother. It sounds as if you're a father."

The dizziness threatened to overtake Bill, and he grabbed the back of a chair.

"You all right, guv?" Darcy moved toward him.

"Just a little lightheaded."

She grinned. "Must run in the family."

Bill moved toward the staircase as if he were wading to it through deep water. He put his hand on the banister but just looked up the stairs. He heard a door open. Charleigh came out, and upon seeing him, her smile grew wide.

"I was just coming to get you. Come along." She motioned him upward, as if encouraging a nervous boy.

The weights that had grounded him released, and he charged up the staircase. She laughed and put a finger to her mouth. "Shhh."

"Oh, uh, sorry." Feeling suddenly awkward, he swallowed as he followed her into the bedroom he shared with his wife. The moment he saw Sarah, all hesitancy vanished.

Her face shimmered with perspiration; her hair was damp and clung to her, but the joy that glowed out of her dark eyes was unmistakable. "Bill." Smiling, she held out her hand to him, and he quickly moved to her side, sitting on the bed. He took her hand in both of his and brought it to his lips, closing his eyes.

"Sarah." He couldn't push anything out beyond that.

"Would you like to see your son?"

Son. Bill's heart went into double-time, and all he could do was nod.

She pulled down the thin sheet that had been protecting the wrapped bundle she held against her side in the crook of her arm. Bill stared in wonder at the tiny face, the closed eyes with their thick lashes. A thatch of dark hair covered his scalp. In awe, he brushed his finger along the baby's head, his soft cheek, to the little hand, which held tightly to a lock of Sarah's hair. How could a baby be so tiny?

Fierce love swamped Bill—for both the little fella who was flesh of their flesh and for his beautiful wife. "He's amazing. And I know the perfect name for him."

She looked at him, expectantly.

"Josiah."

Tears touched her eyes. "He would be honored."

"If it wasn't for your father, none of us would be here right now." His gaze was tender as he looked upon his wife, then down at his son. "Including this little guy."

"Josiah William." Sarah smiled. "It is a good name."

"God has been good to us, Sarah."

"Yes, Bill. He has."

Leaning forward, he touched his lips to hers, thankful for the gentle fragrance of their love.

A Letter To Our Readers

Dear Reader:

In order that we might better contribute to your reading enjoyment, we would appreciate your taking a few minutes to respond to the following questions. We welcome your comments and read each form and letter we receive. When completed, please return to the following:

Fiction Editor
Heartsong Presents
PO Box 719
Uhrichsville, Ohio 44683

1. Did you enjoy reading *A Gentle Fragrance* by Pamela Griffin?
   ❏ Very much! I would like to see more books by this author!
   ❏ Moderately. I would have enjoyed it more if

   _____

   _____

   _____

2. Are you a member of **Heartsong Presents**?   ❏ Yes   ❏ No
   If no, where did you purchase this book? _____

   _____

3. How would you rate, on a scale from 1 (poor) to 5 (superior), the cover design? _____

4. On a scale from 1 (poor) to 10 (superior), please rate the following elements.

   ____ Heroine   ____ Plot
   ____ Hero   ____ Inspirational theme
   ____ Setting   ____ Secondary characters

5. These characters were special because? _____
_____
_____

6. How has this book inspired your life? _____
_____
_____

7. What settings would you like to see covered in future
   Heartsong Presents books? _____
_____
_____

8. What are some inspirational themes you would like to see
   treated in future books? _____
_____
_____

9. Would you be interested in reading other **Heartsong
   Presents** titles? ❏ Yes ❏ No

10. Please check your age range:
    ❏ Under 18   ❏ 18-24
    ❏ 25-34   ❏ 35-45
    ❏ 46-55   ❏ Over 55

Name_____
Occupation_____
Address_____
City, State, Zip_____

NEW MEXICO

3 stories in 1

The stories of three women, struggling with the harsh realities life has thrown their way, play out under the historic mysterious skies of Roswell, New Mexico.

Titles by author Janet Lee Barton include: *A Promise Made*, *A Place Called Home*, and *Making Amends*.

Historical, paperback, 352 pages, 5³⁄₁₆" x 8"

Hearts♥ng

Presents

Great Inspirational Romance at a Great Price!

Heartsong Presents books are inspirational romances in contemporary and historical settings, designed to give you an enjoyable, spirit-lifting reading experience. You can choose wonderfully written titles from some of today's best authors like Peggy Darty, Sally Laity, DiAnn Mills, Colleen L. Reece, Debra White Smith, and many others.

When ordering quantities less than twelve, above titles are $2.97 each.
Not all titles may be available at time of order.

HEARTSONG

P R E S E N T S

If you love Christian romance...

$10.99

You'll love Heartsong Presents' inspiring and faith-filled romances by today's very best Christian authors. . .DiAnn Mills, Wanda E. Brunstetter, and Yvonne Lehman, to mention a few!

When you join Heartsong Presents, you'll enjoy four brand-new, mass market, 176-page books—two contemporary and two historical—that will build you up in your faith when you discover God's role in every relationship you read about!

Imagine. . .four new romances every four weeks—with men and women like you who long to meet the one God has chosen as the love of their lives...all for the low price of $10.99 postpaid.

To join, simply visit www.heartsong presents.com or complete the coupon below and mail it to the address provided.

Mass Market 176 Pages

✂- -

YES! Sign me up for Heart♥ng!

NEW MEMBERSHIPS WILL BE SHIPPED IMMEDIATELY!
Send no money now. We'll bill you only $10.99 postpaid with your first shipment of four books. Or for faster action, call 1-740-922-7280.

NAME_____

ADDRESS_____

CITY_____ STATE _____ ZIP _____

MAIL TO: HEARTSONG PRESENTS, P.O. Box 721, Uhrichsville, Ohio 44683
or sign up at WWW.HEARTSONGPRESENTS.COM